THE GOBLIN HORDE

THE BRAMBLE

THE CABIN

THE DEEP DARK

HINKYPUNK PATH

THE ODDMIRE

BAD BERRIES

HIDDEN GOBLIN PATH

THE
OĐĐMIRE

BOOK ONE

CHANGELING

THE
OƊƊMIRE

BOOK ONE

CHANGELING

written and illustrated by

William Ritter

Algonquin Young Readers   2019

Published by
Algonquin Young Readers
an imprint of Algonquin Books of Chapel Hill
Post Office Box 2225
Chapel Hill, North Carolina 27515-2225
a division of
Workman Publishing
225 Varick Street
New York, New York 10014

Design by Carla Weise.

LIBRARY OF CONGRESS CATALOGING-IN-PUBLICATION DATA

Names: Ritter, William, author.
Title: Changeling / William Ritter.
Description: First edition. | Chapel Hill, North Carolina : Algonquin Young
Readers, 2019. | Series: Oddmire ; book one | Summary: Twelve-year-olds Tinn
and Cole, raised as human twins in sleepy Endsborough, risk their lives in the
Wild Wood, Oddmire Swamp, and the Deep Dark to learn which is a goblin
changeling with an important mission.
Identifiers: LCCN 2018033941 | ISBN 9781616208394 (hardcover : alk. paper)
Subjects: | CYAC: Changelings—Fiction. | Twins—Fiction. | Brothers—Fiction. |
Adventure and adventurers—Fiction. | Magic—Fiction. | Fantasy.
Classification: LCC PZ7.R516 Ch 2019 | DDC [Fic]—dc23
LC record available at https://lccn.loc.gov/2018033941

10 9 8 7 6 5 4 3 2 1
First Edition

For Justin and Jack,
always.

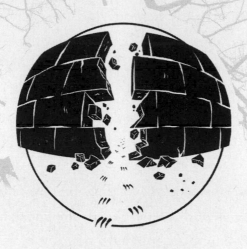

PROLOGUE

A VERY LONG TIME AGO, HUMANS AND FAIRIES and elves and dolphins and all of the other intelligent beings of the world got sick of one another—which was understandable, as intelligent beings were all pretty much rubbish in those days. After much arguing, they decided to split up the world and build a sort of magical wall between the two halves. On the human side of the barrier, life would be governed by logic and reason and the laws of nature. It would be an honest world of soil and struggle. The other side would be ruled by forces more ancient than any earthly science, a world of magic and madness and raw potential. Humans called their side the Earth, and magical beings called their side the Annwyn (all except for the gnomes, who called it Pippin-Gilliewhipple—which is one of many reasons that, to this day, nobody from either side much cares for gnomes).

For many centuries, the wall stood—a sort of veil between two worlds, invisible but everywhere. Neither side could see or touch the other, and in time many creatures forgot there was another world at all. This remained the state of things until rogue groups brought their simmering strife to an unruly boil and a new war broke out. As it turned out, intelligent beings were still fairly rubbish if not properly supervised. The resulting battle blasted a great, gaping hole right through the invisible barrier.

When the dust had settled, some felt the hole in the wall should be patched back up, and others felt the barrier should come down entirely. In all the hubbub, nobody noticed as the thing that had been *inside* the wall—the thing that may have been the very *soul* of the wall—escaped. Nobody was watching as the thing that had spent countless centuries listening at the cracks and growing hungrier and hungrier slipped past the rubble and across the bloody battlefield. Nobody saw it slide quietly into the forest.

The Thing clutched at shadows as it moved between the trees, drawing the darkness around itself like a riding cloak. It had never known sunlight, or birdsong, or honey-sweet breezes, or even the sound of its own name. If the Thing even had ever had a name, it had never had anyone to speak it.

The Thing whipped past mossy boulders, through towering trees, and over the muggy, murky Oddmire. When it reached the very heart of the Wild Wood, it finally slowed and came to rest. The trees grew more densely there, and the air was still. Even the sound of the birds died away. The shadows here were thick and heavy, and the Thing gathered them up, greedily.

The Thing knew shadows. In that sunless, starless place between worlds, there had been shadows so absolute they had no form. The Thing's whole world had been a shadow—its whole life had been one great shadow, and within it, the Thing had felt impossibly small. But the shadows in this new place were different. They would do as it bid them. They were powerful, those shadows of stones and boulders and tall pine trees, and the pieces torn from them felt comfortable as they knit together across the Thing's back. The Thing felt strong. Beneath its swelling cloak of darkness, the Thing began to take on new shapes. Bigger shapes. Terrible shapes. Still, there was one shadow that caught the Thing like a thorn: its own. The creature's meager slip of a shadow followed it, clung to it, taunted it with its own true, trifling form.

The creature plunged its talons into the forest floor, and for a time, the only sound was the scratching of unseen claws digging into the soil. When the hole was deep enough, the Thing turned its talons in on itself. It tore and it ripped until finally, reverently, it lowered its own severed shadow into the cold earth and buried the humble scrap beneath the dirt. All around it, pools of darkness blossomed as if the entire forest floor were a fresh, clean napkin laid over a seeping ink stain.

The darkness grew.

The Thing drew itself up to its full height, and then it drew itself up a little higher, and higher still. Countless stolen shadows rippled along its cloak like waves of grain shimmering in a breeze. The Thing would be whatever it pleased now. It was never going back.

The darkness spreading across the forest floor solidified into angry coils and knots as it grew. Wicked thorns burst from its surface. For just a moment, there was silence and the forest was still. And then the darkness began to creep.

ONE

THE TOWN OF ENDSBOROUGH WAS A QUAINT community teetering on the edge of what could be only generously termed civilization. A dense forest known by the locals as the Wild Wood curled around the town the way a Great Dane might curl around a terrier puppy. A single, winding road was all that connected the people of Endsborough to the rest of the world. Two days' ride on a sturdy horse would take travelers past Cobb's Outpost and to the crowded city of Glanville, where modernity was all the rage. Gas lamps were on their way out in Glanville, and fancy electric streetlights were on their way in. Quiet Endsborough, meanwhile, had not yet gotten around to gas. Its citizens had adopted the practical habit of going to sleep when the sun went down—and when the sun rose, they rose with it. There was a straightforward simplicity to Endsborough.

The town boasted a lumber mill and a coal mine. It had modest apple orchards and more cows than it really needed, if it was being honest. In its middle sat a brick building that served as the schoolhouse on weekdays, the church on Sundays, and the meeting hall on Saturdays. It was a no-nonsense sort of town that heard about notions like technology and progress and decided that they sounded exhausting.

Everybody knew the wood was home to monsters: towering giants and trolls and goblins who kidnapped sweet, dimpled babies in the dead of night, stealing them away into the forest forever. Daring adventures awaited any hero brave enough to cross that tree line and march into the unknown. Which was why the people of Endsborough did not. Endsborough was simply not the sort of town that went looking for trouble. Trouble, however, found its own way to Endsborough.

Trouble crept silently out of the Wild Wood one warm summer night, holding its breath as it tiptoed toward a cottage on the edge of town. Trouble listened outside the back window, waiting patiently until everyone inside was asleep.

And then, when it was quite certain it would not be spotted, trouble made its move.

Kull tiptoed along the back wall, holding his precious bundle close to his chest as he hurried from shadow to shadow. He meant well—mostly—at least by goblin standards. His pointed ears perked up at every sound, and his jagged teeth ground nervously against one another.

It wasn't treason, what he was doing. It was tradition. And it was necessary. True, the goblin chief had commanded that the human world was now strictly off-limits, and yes, there had been talk of terrible shame and torture, and something about entrails, for any member of the goblin horde who trespassed into the world of men—but the quiet, dark room into which Kull crept that night did not belong to a *man*, did it? A *man* could hardly fit in the wee cradle or appreciate the colorful rattle and the fluffy stuffed lamb, could he?

Kull was going to steal that baby. Stealing babies was what goblins did. Or it was what they ought to do. It was certainly what they *used* to do.

Kull grunted as he pulled himself up to the open window with one hand, the bundle still cradled tight in the other. Perhaps *not* stealing babies was what had gotten the horde into its current sad state of affairs. Chief Nudd was

7

too soft. He was too modern-minded. He was too weak. Yes, he threatened to boil their noses and braid their toes from time to time, but he so rarely followed through on those threats anymore. Too much time spent colluding with humans, that was the problem. Not enough time spent stealing babies.

Kull slipped down from the window to the floorboards as quietly as he could. The air in the room smelled of soap and talcum powder.

The chief's empathetic quirks had been tolerable while the horde was thriving, but things were different now. Kull felt it. The chief felt it. Every goblin in the horde felt it. Slowly but steadily, magic was leaving the Wild Wood. Slowly but steadily, the horde was dying. It was one thing to sit idly by when there was nothing to be done about it, but it was something else entirely to sit idly by when the solution was right there in their hands.

The cloth bundle shifted against Kull's grip, and he felt tiny, soft fingers wrap around his thumb. He glanced down at the bundle in his arms. His throat felt dry. The changeling was the answer.

A changeling was more than just a goblin who could transform to look like a human. A changeling was the living embodiment of goblin magic. It was a symbol of power and potential. It was hope. It was no coincidence that the changeling had been born just when things appeared most dire. Chief Nudd had failed them, but out of his failure, the one shining light was this baby.

The horde had not produced a changeling—a real changeling, not just an ordinary goblin in a wig and a dress—since the era of the Manky Basilisk. Nudd's father had still been chief back then. The old chief would never have questioned what to do when a changeling was born into the horde. He had been a goblin's goblin, steeped in the Old Ways. Now that he was gone, somebody had to see that the Old Ways did not go forgotten.

Admittedly, if Kull was being truthful, he only half remembered the Old Ways himself. Many of them he had never learned in the first place, but he would bleed for the bits he did remember—well, someone would bleed, anyway—and Chief Nudd and all the rest of them would thank him when it was done. Until then, he was on his own. If Kull hoped to see the ancient traditions revived, he would have to sort out the details by himself, and he would have to sort them out quickly.

The squishy pink baby in the crib ahead of him was already beginning to stir. Kull hoped to whisk the little human back into the Wild Wood before it started crying, leaving the changeling in its stead. Then there would be the customary exchange with the fair folk—Kull would have to dig out the ancient contracts to find the details on that. He couldn't remember exactly how it all worked—but soon enough the human baby would be on the other side of the veil and magic would return to this one. How long should the changeling remain with the humans? It had a three in it, Kull thought. Or maybe a seven? It was important, he remembered that much. Pesky details about numbers and ceremonies and proper procedures could wait until after he had stolen the child and returned home in glory.

It wasn't about abducting children, Kull reminded himself, or about the merry havoc the little changeling would wreak in its place. It was about the good of the horde. It was about tradition. Goblinkind needed magic. Just a little. Just enough. They needed to tap into the ancient rituals. They needed the Old Ways. They needed that baby.

Kull clambered up into the bassinet with his bundle and set the squirming changeling down gently in the soft bedding. It was the rarest of their kind in a generation, and Kull would see it fulfill its purpose before Nudd could geld its beautiful mischief. In his hands it had looked at least mostly goblin, albeit a goblin with skin like smoke and shadows, but now it rippled and wavered like a living mirage. Its skin was speckled with stars and peeling like old wallpaper, and then it was the color of the cherrywood crib and as woolly as the child's blanket.

Kull had been nervous that the transformation would not work without the proper words, but now he grinned with all his jagged teeth to see the thing's magical instincts taking over.

Somewhere inside the house, a floorboard creaked. Kull froze, all of his senses instantly trained on the door to the hallway. He should have latched it. It hung ajar, and now soft footfalls were approaching. A flicker of shadow. Kull's breath caught in his throat and his eyes went wide.

The door shuddered inward and a fat black cat sauntered in. It glanced up at Kull, who stood motionless inside the bassinet, and then it sat down on the carpet to watch, flicking its tail and looking unimpressed.

Kull breathed. It was fine. The full-grown humans were still asleep. He turned back around to bear witness to the glorious miracle of his proud and ancient culture. Two button-nosed babies with pudgy pink cheeks blinked back at him.

It was done! The changeling had performed beyond Kull's wildest imagination; the impersonation was exact! Kull had only to pluck the helpless infant from the safety of its bed and secrete it away into the Deep Dark, leaving the doppelgänger in its place. First one child smacked its tiny lips and then the other. The other rubbed its cheek and then the first.

Kull hesitated. He peered at the squishy little face closest to him. He peered at the other face. Which was it? He nudged the first child with a bony knuckle. As one, the babies began to cry. Kull cringed.

Up the hall, a door clicked open, and a woman's tired voice echoed down the corridor. "He's probably just hungry. You sleep. I'll put him back to bed."

Kull panicked. He took the closest child into his shaking hands, and then dropped it and wrapped his fingers around the farthest instead. The babies wailed and kicked their chubby legs. Kull's chest was pounding. Which one was it?

He hopped from one foot to the other. The sound of footsteps drew nearer. Which one? Which one? He glanced from the door to the children to the door to the children to . . .

The door opened with a mewl like a kitten. "Hush, sweetie. Mama's here," Mrs. Burton cooed blearily. The curtain flapped in the cool night breeze as she crossed to the crib. Mrs. Burton froze. Mrs. Burton stared.

Kull had already burst through the underbrush and into the Wild Wood when the lamps flickered on in the house behind him. His feet were racing, his heart was thudding, his head was full, and his hands were empty.

TWO

Twins.

Annie Burton distinctly remembered giving birth to one baby. One. She had been there. She had counted. Ten fingers, ten toes, one baby. But now . . . twins.

There had been a great deal of talk that first morning, and it was scarcely midday before the house had filled with noisy onlookers. Father Lewis had brought rosaries. Old Jim had tossed salt all over the house. Nosy Mrs. Grouse from across the road had been the first to say the word aloud.

"Goblins. It's goblins, I swear. They've stolen a baby before, you know. From right here in Endsborough. They

13

used to talk about it all the time. My grandmother knew the family."

"Helen, please—" Annie began, but Mrs. Grouse ignored her.

"Once upon a time, there was a child whom the goblins stole away. That's how the story goes. She was a beautiful child with joyful dimples and thick curls of rich brown hair, and the goblins came and they just took her away."

"When I was growing up, it was fairies," said Old Jim Warner.

"No. It was the goblins," Mrs. Grouse continued forcefully, "and they left one of their own in place of the child, a changeling. It was an awful thing—a monster in disguise. For three days the child's parents fed the vile little creature, fretted over it, thinking it was their own flesh and blood. Then, one morning, the goblin could hide no longer. It struck. Tore up the nursery, shrieked like the devil, and when the frightened parents came running, it killed the husband dead while his poor wife watched. Drove her mad to see it. She chased the evil thing into the forest, so they say, and she never came back out again."

"You've got your stories all mixed up," Old Jim grumbled. "That's the legend of the Witch of the Wild Wood. And she never had a husband in the first place. She was a single mother and the fairies came and stole away her only daughter, but nobody in town believed her. Then, when she went into the forest to try to get her baby back, the fairies cursed her to wander the Deep Dark forever, snatching up wayward children in place of her own."

"It was goblins," Mrs. Grouse asserted.

"Fairies," huffed Old Jim.

"You're both talking about fairy tales," said Annie Burton. "This is madness! They're not monsters. They're just children."

"*One* of them is," said Mrs. Grouse.

"If there really is a witch in the woods," Joseph Burton said, his face stoic, "and she lost her baby to . . . to magical creatures, then maybe she's still out there. Maybe she would know how to recognize a changeling."

"There is no witch in the woods," said Father Lewis. It was the first time the old man had spoken since his arrival, and his voice was low and soft. "There never was a witch. There was just a woman."

The room was silent as all eyes turned to the aging pastor.

"The stories are wrong," he continued. "There was a woman who used to live alone in the woods, that much is true. I don't know anything about fairies or goblins or any of that—I think it was just regular old grief that sent her out there. I met her, just once, when I was still a young man.

I went walking along a path in the forest and got turned around. The woman was real, and she was sad. She had indeed suffered a great loss. The poor old thing just wanted to be left alone."

"But if there's truth to any of it . . ." Joseph Burton allowed the words to trail off. His eyes were on the back window and the swaying trees.

"The woman was already quite old back then," said the pastor gently. "I'm sure she's long passed by now, God rest her. That hasn't stopped the stories about that poor lady from growing into absolute nonsense."

"It's not nonsense," mumbled Old Jim.

For once, Mrs. Grouse seemed to agree with him. "Indeed it's not. Proof enough is in that bassinet," she insisted. "It isn't natural. Isn't right. It's goblins, I swear. It's a changeling."

Nobody wanted to agree with the superstitious woman, but nobody could truly say she was wrong, either. You couldn't live your life beside the Wild Wood and not believe at least a few of the old stories.

They burned sage and poked both children with silver, but the babies only sneezed and giggled and batted at the spoons. Nobody in town was quite certain what to look for in a changeling. Eventually, somebody got the idea to send away for advice from an expert they had heard about

16

out in New Fiddleham. *Iron*—the expert advised them by post—*touch the child with iron within the first three days.* By the time this counsel arrived, seven days had passed. They tried anyway, but both babies just grappled at the fireplace poker and got soot all over their swaddling clothes.

And so, after a week of dithering and debating, it was decided (for lack of a better option) that they would simply have to wait. The goblin child would reveal its own true nature eventually. A goblin, after all, couldn't resist getting up to all manner of mischief. They would just have to be wary and watchful. Until then, the Burtons would care for both boys as their own.

Bit by bit, the neighbors ceased stopping by to gawk and speculate until, one evening, only Mrs. Grouse remained. "A goblin, Annie," she reminded her, unnecessarily, before she left for the night. "A horrible goblin changeling, sleeping side by side with your own flesh and blood."

"Good night, Helen."

The boys were indeed sleeping side by side as Annie closed the door behind her. Annie could not help but notice that her own baby—whichever one it was—had slept more soundly since the arrival of his mysterious twin. They seemed equally calmed by each other's presence and distressed by their separation. They would cry ceaselessly when she attempted to move them into different rooms, but quieted at once when they were back in each other's company, until soon they would be snoring peacefully. She watched them for a long time, listening to the soft rhythm of their breathing.

Until the changeling's natural mischief gave the wicked thing away, she would let the matter rest, along with the boys. *Her* boys.

No reason to rush the matter, Annie thought, taking a deep breath. After all, they would know the truth soon enough.

THREE

It had been twelve years, eleven months, and twenty-eight days since Annie Burton's baby had mysteriously become two babies. By now she had learned what more experienced parents could have told her as a young mother: mischief is in the nature of goblins and growing children in roughly equal measure, which left the matter uncertain far longer than she had anticipated.

Annie Burton was not the sort of woman to be thwarted by a little twist of fate. Fate, it seemed, had taken this as a challenge. It had been twelve years, eleven months, and twenty-*one* days since Annie Burton had become a widow.

Some of the gossips in town considered her less a widow and more an abandoned wife—Joseph Burton had clearly left work alive that night and simply never arrived back home—but Annie refused to believe her husband would leave her alone with two crying, kicking, grappling, growing baby boys for anything less than his own demise. Annie knew she was a widow. The way that she said it, with her jaw set and her eyes tense and narrow, made the towns-people hope, for her husband's sake, that she was right.

Annie wiped the sweat from her brow and pulled with both hands. The long, stubborn blackberry vine in her grip finally ripped free, its roots giving up their hold. Annie took a deep, satisfied breath and tugged, unwinding the perni-cious thing from the slats in her back fence. When she and Joseph had moved into the little cottage, the plant had been growing right up to their back door. Inch by inch, year by year, she had cut the vines back. As the boys had grown older, they had begun to help her, chopping at the bram-bles like knights battling a thorny dragon, and together they kept the vines at bay. Annie now stood in the wide garden that they had grown where the persistent plant had once held dominion. The plot of land had been hard won, and she was not about to let the prickly brute reclaim it.

She tossed the vanquished vine on the heap with the others. Its thin, wispy end whipped toward her as she threw it, catching her a scratch across the neck with its tiny barbs. She gritted her teeth and glowered at the fallen plant. "Was that really necessary?" she said.

As if in reply, voices carried across the grass from the front of the house. Annie recognized their cadence long before they were close enough for her to make out their words. Dusting her hands off on her apron, she gave the garden one last look before her boys came tumbling through it, then braced herself for the inevitable fistfuls of tadpoles, chronicles of skinned knees (they always came in twos with her boys), or, worse: the flood of excuses about whichever neighbor was likely to come around soon with wild accusations about something that was definitely, absolutely, positively *not* the twins' fault.

"—gotta go back, then," one of the boys was saying as they neared.

"That is a *terrible* idea," the other replied.

"What's a terrible idea?" Annie asked as her boys came around the corner.

"Hi, Mom!" Cole said, a little more loudly than was strictly necessary.

"The garden looks really good, Mom," Tinn added. "You want some help?"

"I want to know what's a terrible idea."

The twins glanced at each other.

21

"Yams," said Cole.

"Catapult," said Tinn at the same time.

"Yam catapult," said Cole. "Terrible idea."

Tinn nodded. "Waste of good vegetables."

Annie sighed. "And that is exactly the reason I kicked the two of you out of the garden this morning. What have you been up to?"

"Just playing in our climbing tree out by the creek," said Cole.

Annie glanced at Tinn, one eyebrow raised.

"Yep. Out by the creek. We were about to go back. I . . ." Tinn's eyes flickered to Cole and back. "I forgot my hat."

"You swear to me you haven't been anywhere near the mill this time?" Annie pressed. "Or down into the quarry?"

"No, ma'am," the boys said together.

Annie looked suspiciously from Tinn to Cole. "You promise to behave yourselves?"

As one, the boys grinned and nodded.

Annie Burton sighed the heavy sigh of a mother who knows her children far too well and somehow loves them anyway. "I expect you back before sundown," she said, though she said the final word to the boys' backs as they scampered away.

"Love you, Mom!" they called over their shoulders in unison.

"Don't you dare go into Old Jim's orchard, either!" Annie yelled after them. "I don't want to hear one word about you two trespassing again! You know how that man gets."

"We would never!" Cole called back earnestly, dashing around the corner of the house.

"We know the rules!" yelled Tinn, one step behind his brother.

Ten minutes later, the boys rounded the bend to Old Jim's orchard. The path was lined with old, twisty, knobby trees.

"This really is a terrible idea," whispered Tinn.

"Yup. Shoulda thought of that before you went and left your hat in a stupid apple tree," Cole replied.

"It's not like I did it on purpose!" Tinn groused. "Old Jim almost caught me. I barely got down in time. Skinned my shin real bad on the way."

"Tree got yours? Mine got all tore up on the fence."

They paused to pull up their pant legs and compare wounds. For as long as they could remember, the twins had not only looked the same, they had always managed to sustain identical injuries. When one cut his finger on a nail, the other would invariably have a run-in with the cat's claws or a broken glass.

Tinn grumbled as he pulled his cuff back down. "This is *your* fault."

"Yeah, well. It's *your* hat," said Cole. "If we *don't* sneak back in and get it, then Old Jim's gonna find it, and you just know he'll tell Mom. If you don't wanna get in trouble for sneaking in again, then we *gotta* sneak back in again."

"You're such a dummy."

"Yeah, well—I'm the dummy with a hat."

"You could at least pretend you're not enjoying this."

Cole just grinned and walked a little faster.

They rounded the last turn and jolted to a stop. Ahead of them, not a hundred feet away, Old Jim himself was bent over a fallen piece of his weathered fence. The twins ducked behind the nearest tree to hide.

"I've got an idea," whispered Cole.

"No," said Tinn.

"Aw, come on. He hasn't seen us yet," said Cole.

"No," said Tinn.

"Let's do it just like last Thanksgiving," said Cole, his eyes bright. He peered around the tree trunk.

"We got grounded for a week for last Thanksgiving," hissed Tinn. "And I still have cranberry stains on my shoes."

"Fine. Not *exactly* like last Thanksgiving. He's not looking—here we go!" Cole darted across the path, taking cover behind another tree, twenty feet closer to Jim's orchard.

Tinn swallowed nervously. He peered around the tree trunk and down the path. Old Jim was still facing away,

24

rummaging about in a battered wooden toolbox. Tinn felt the familiar twisting in his stomach. He glanced over at Cole. He could almost feel the energy rippling off his brother. Cole kept his head low—if he had been a cat, his tail would have been twitching. He gave Tinn an enthusiastic thumbs-up, and Tinn tried very hard not to smile. Smiling only encouraged his brother. Cole was doing this, and if Cole was doing it, then Tinn was doing it.

As quietly as he could, Tinn stepped out from behind the tree.

Old Jim turned around.

"Who's that?" the farmer called, straightening.

"Just me," said Tinn, trying to walk as nonchalantly as he could. He stumbled, and then laughed nervously. His palms already felt sweaty. What did he normally do with his hands when he was walking? He was pretty sure he wasn't doing it now.

"*Me* who?" the old man barked.

Out of the corner of his eye, Tinn saw Cole grinning up at him before he disappeared behind a bush. "It's Tinn, sir. Burton. Annie Burton's boy. Just out walking. Um. How are you, today, sir?"

Old Jim's eyes narrowed. "Where's that brother of yours?"

"He's . . . at home," Tinn lied.

"Hmph. The two of you are thick as thieves." Old Jim's eyes scanned the path. Tinn was certain his gaze lingered as it passed over the bush where Cole was concealed.

"He got scared," Tinn blurted. "He got scared and ran home."

Jim's bushy gray eyebrows rose and he turned back to Tinn. "That so? Scared of what?"

"Of . . . of something we saw while we were playing near the Wild Wood earlier," Tinn bluffed. He knew at once that he had chosen the right approach. The farmer's jaw set and his head rose. Nobody in town had more stories about the things that lurked in the Wild Wood than Old Jim.

"That so? What'd y'all see?"

Tinn stepped closer, keeping Old Jim's eyes on him and away from Cole. "Oh, um, I'm not sure, sir. Something . . . tall?" His voice caught in his throat for a moment as Cole tiptoed across the grass, not ten feet behind Old Jim.

"Tall?"

"Tall. Yes, sir. Tall. With, um, eyes. Cole got real scared of it. He's kind of a scaredy-cat about stuff like that. Big coward. Kind of a baby."

From behind Old Jim, Cole stuck out his tongue at Tinn and then silently vaulted the fence. Tinn tried not to let his eyes follow Cole as his brother slipped behind the nearest tree in the orchard.

"And you ain't scared?" the old man said.

"Huh?" said Tinn. "No. I mean, I'm not scared. I'm sure it was nothing, really. I ain't afraid of the woods."

"You should be." Old Jim's eyes bore into Tinn until he began to feel uncomfortable. "You ever gone into those woods?"

"Sure," said Tinn, smiling nervously. "Loads of times. Mom lets us pick sassafras near the old bridge."

"I'm not talking about the tree line, kid. I mean the woods proper. There are creatures that live in those woods that you won't learn about in your schoolbooks. You ever been as far in as the Oddmire?"

Tinn shook his head. Over Jim's shoulder he could see Cole shinnying up the apple tree. He gulped and shook his head. "The Oddmire. That—that's the swampy part, right?" Keep him talking. Keep him distracted.

"The Oddmire ain't no ordinary swamp, kid," Old Jim said. "It will grab hold of you, turn you around, pull you down. That's not all. The mire divides the Wild Wood in two. There's plenty to be nervous about on this side, but the deeper you go, the worse it gets. If you manage to make it beyond the Oddmire, the woods only get thicker. The trees grow closer. The woodsmen who used to haul lumber through these parts named it the Deep Dark. Even if they could find their way past the mire, loggers knew better than to take a tree from the Deep Dark. Cursed wood. That forest changes a person. A fellow don't come out of the Deep Dark the same man who went in." Again, the old man's eyes bore into Tinn.

"Have *you* ever been to the Deep Dark, sir?" Tinn's voice came out like a whisper.

Old Jim's icy gaze rose and his lips turned up in a sneer. "At the very heart of the Wild Wood, past the Oddmire, in the thickest part of the Deep Dark, they say there's a nest of thorny vines so dense and sharp they catch anything fool enough to stumble into their grip. Not even light escapes from the bramble."

Tinn barely noticed that Cole had climbed out onto the limb of the apple tree behind Jim. Tinn's forgotten hat was hanging inches away from Cole's fingertips.

"So," Old Jim concluded, slapping his tool chest closed, "next time your brother decides he's scared of whatever's watching from those woods and he goes running home, you'd be wise to join him."

Tinn's eyes shot from the old man to Cole, who was suddenly dangling from the branch in plain sight with the hat clutched in one fist. He grinned triumphantly and waggled the hat at Tinn until he almost lost his grip, swinging wildly for a moment before catching hold of the branch again with both hands.

Old Jim sniffed and spat, then began to turn back toward the orchard. Cole froze, trapped where he hung.

"Wait!" Tinn said.

Old Jim paused and raised a bushy eyebrow.

"What, um, what do *you* think it was?" Tinn asked. "What do you think might have been watching us from the woods?"

"Hm." Jim nodded sagely. "All kinds of ghouls and odd-lings in those woods. People used to say that the founders brought the spirits of the old country with them when they moved to Endsborough."

"*Spirits of the old country* doesn't sound so bad."

"There's a reason the founders *left* the old country, kid. Still, if there's one thing you best hope is *not* watching you from the Wild Wood, it's the queen."

Tinn shuddered. He hated these stories. The Queen of the Deep Dark. Mother of Monsters. The Witch of the Wild Wood.

"Some say she eats errant children," Jim continued. "Others say she turns them into wild animals. Some say that she can transform at will into a wild animal herself, her cloak becoming the hide of a great beast. Some people say she planted the bramble, years ago—or else the vines are her terrible fingers, reaching out to snatch boys and girls who tread too far into her forest."

A tree branch cracked like a rifle shot and Tinn jumped. His heart was pounding. He had lost track of Cole, and now he couldn't see him anywhere.

Old Jim spun around, scowling, and plodded into the orchard. Tinn's mouth opened and closed, but he could think of nothing more to say to stall the farmer. Step by agonizing step, Old Jim stalked up to the tree. And then around it. And back. "Damn deer," he cussed. "They knocked down my fence just this morning. Looks like they've been helping themselves to my apples again."

Tinn let out his breath.

"Hi!" called a voice from behind him.

For the second time, Tinn jumped. Cole laughed as he came jogging up the path.

"Cole, I—you . . ."

"I just got back." Cole winked. "From *home*."

"Right. Yes! Because you were at home."

"I brought your hat, dummy. We really should get going."

"Right. Yeah. Well, have a good day, sir. Sorry about the . . . the deer."

Old Jim grumbled and shook his head as he watched the boys jog away.

FOUR

"You almost got caught," said Tinn, punching his brother in the arm. "*We* almost got caught!"

Cole chuckled. "It's not fun unless you almost get caught."

"No, it's way more fun *without* getting caught. And way less scary. Old Jim gives me the heebie-jeebies." Tinn couldn't help but keep glancing out at the tree line as they walked along the forest's edge. "How come you always gotta push your luck, anyway?"

"I dunno." Cole kicked a dirt clod. "It just feels good to prove you can, I guess. Like you're special. Don't you ever feel like you've got something hiding inside you that you just wanna . . ." Cole trailed off. "You know." They walked on in silence for several paces.

Tinn knew. Everybody knew. They knew, but they didn't *know*. The boys had grown up surrounded by stories about fair folk and oddlings—and the story that the boys knew most intimately was the story of them, the story of what was hiding inside one of them. Sometimes Tinn could swear he felt it prickling just under his skin. Sometimes Cole was sure it was humming in his bones. They both wondered if they were the one. They both worried.

"I just want to be special sometimes," Cole said suddenly. "I want to be a hero, like Hercules doing all those labors we had to read about for Mrs. Silva's class. I just want to prove I can do—I don't know—big things. Scary things."

"Hercules was a twin, too," Tinn recalled. "He had a brother called Isosceles or something. No, Iphicles."

"I don't think I read that part," said Cole. "Did his brother get to go on cool adventures and kill monsters and stuff, too?"

"Um . . . I don't think so," said Tinn. "Maybe? He wasn't a demigod like Hercules. I think he was just a person."

The stream was up ahead, and Cole began scooping up pebbles as they walked. Tinn leaned down to pick up a few, too.

"Do you think he wanted to?" said Tinn.

"Who wanted to what?" said Cole, picking bits of bark out of his handful of rocks.

"The brother. Do you think he wanted to fight monsters and stuff?"

"Of course he did. Why wouldn't he?" Cole asked.

"Well, I mean—Hercules didn't really want to do any of it, did he? He didn't want to wrestle lions or kill Amazons or clean poop out of an old stable. He just did it to make up for some really bad stuff in his past. He just wanted to go home. I don't think he ever wanted to be a hero at all—I think he just wanted to not be a monster."

They listened to the sound of their own footsteps scuffling along the dusty path for a while.

"Hercules didn't clean poop," said Cole.

"Did so. It was one of the labors."

"That's gross." Cole laughed.

"You're gross."

They drew up to the bridge and Cole nodded. "Ready?"

Tinn shifted the pebbles in his palm. "Three . . . two . . . one . . ."

They tossed all the pebbles at once high into the air and watched as they came down with a satisfying *plip-plip-plippity-SPLASH-plip-ploop* into the stream. Cole leaned over the railing to watch the cloud of sediment drifting up under the water's surface. "Maybe Hercules would have liked doing his labors more if he had brought his brother with him," Cole said.

Tinn did not reply. His gaze was on the forest. Just as the boys had thrown their pebbles, he had caught sight of something. There—in the shadows at the forest's edge—had been a pair of eyes, watching from between the leaves of a wide bush. The bush swayed and then was still.

Tinn swallowed. He wanted to go home.

FIVE

KULL FIDGETED WITH THE LITTLE SQUARE OF parchment as he hurried between the trees. Already he had folded and unfolded the thing so many times it was beginning to get soft at the edges.

It did not feel as heavy as it should. It was only paper and ink, but its message had felt like lead in his chest for so long. How many nights had he glowered at that paper, leaning his jaw on one tight fist as he dipped his pen into the inkwell? How many books and scrolls had he amassed—goblin lore and human stories, and even a handful of fairy tales—stacks and heaps and piles that loomed around him as he wrote? His head still ached from study.

Kull had always fancied himself a problem solver, but he preferred the problems that could be solved the traditional way, through violence or theft or running away. This problem had been different. It had required *words*.

Kull paused under a viny tree and took a deep breath. Bugs buzzed around him, and from just beyond the bushes, a stream burbled. He had almost reached the human village when from ahead of him came the sound of voices. Kull knew those voices better than he knew his own. As quietly as he could, he crept to the edge of the tree line.

With one hand, he delicately pushed aside the leaves and peered between them. The boys were at the bridge. He could not quite make out their words over the trickle of the stream, but he knew the scene well enough; he had been watching the twins from the bushes all their lives.

In a moment they would leave the bridge and continue up the winding dirt path, past a thick oak tree. They always stopped at the big oak tree on their way home. They called it their climbing tree. Kull's hand holding the note felt clammy. The tree was the place. He would leave the message in the tree.

As one, the boys suddenly threw their handfuls of pebbles into the air, and Kull flinched. They would soon be moving on. He let the leaves settle back into place and took off across the forest as quickly as his goblin feet could carry him. He needed to reach that tree before they did.

Words. Kull had been practicing human words for months. He had been forced to; the children had disregarded every note he had left for them in Goblish over the years.

Once, when the boys were seven, he had gotten brazen and carved the whole message out as clear as day on their windowsill. The boys had rubbed their fingers over his careful Goblish script and mused aloud about how the cat must have gotten stuck outside and clawed up the wood trying to climb in through the window. If only Kull had been allowed to cross the forest line and just speak directly to the children—but he was bound by his blood pact, and bend the rules all he might, he could not break them. Human English was simple enough to speak. Every goblin learns how to haggle in the seven sacred trade tongues before they reach gambling age. Writing was different. Writing was hard. But the boys needed to know what he knew. They needed to believe him. He needed them to believe.

So he had written the message at last in the fashion of men, using words that humans knew. They were good words, he was sure of it. He had stolen them from books and learned them by heart in their strange, curvy human script.

His pen had scratched them out along the rough parchment, his lips moving silently as he drew each slow letter. *Once . . . upon . . . a . . . time . . .*

They felt like important words.

"You think it really was the witch?" Cole said. "You think the Queen of the Deep Dark is watching us?" He swung his leg up onto the first branch of the knotty climbing tree and pulled himself to sitting.

"No," said Tinn. He wished he had not told his brother about what he had seen in the forest. Or what he thought he had seen. He had been listening to Old Jim for too long. "It was probably nothing." He wrapped his hands around the branch and clambered up to join Cole.

"Do you think she's real?" Cole asked. "I mean—even if you didn't see her, I figure she's really in there somewhere, right? Lots of folks have stories about her. That means she's probably real, right?"

"I don't know. I don't think so. If I was a witch and I could do magic and fly on a broom and stuff, I wouldn't spend my time stealing children and killing crops and things."

"I can think of a few people I would turn into frogs," said Cole.

"Hey, what's that?" Tinn pointed to the little knothole in the middle of the tree. Poking out of it was a dust-brown piece of paper. He had almost mistaken it for a leaf.

"Another one?" Cole plucked it out. It had been almost a year since the last scrap of parchment had found its way into their tree, covered in scratchy little ink lines. The boys had spent an afternoon imagining it was a secret code and that they were spies who could crack it. When they had shown it to their mother, she had guessed it was just someone's spare blotting paper. "Huh," Cole said, turning it over. "It's got our names on it."

Tinn glanced up and down the dusty path, and then into the shadows of the forest. There was nobody else in sight. It was just Cole and him and the gnarled climbing tree.

And the note.

Cole unfolded it. "Who d'you think left it?" he whispered.

"What's it say?" Tinn leaned in over his brother's shoulder, looking at the unsteady cursive.

Once upon a time, there was a child whom the goblins came to steal, and once upon a time, there was a child whom the goblins left behind . . .

39

Kull's heart was racing. He watched over the fronds of a bushy fern as the twins unfolded his note. Absently, he mouthed the words as they read it.

Once upon a time, there was a child whom the goblins came to steal, and once upon a time, there was a child whom the goblins left behind. Once upon a time, there was a fool who thought he knew best, and once upon a time, there were children who needed to know more.

Firstly, little human, it was me. I tried to kidnap you and sell you to the fairies, and I am sorry. Even though you would have loved it, and it would have solved a lot of problems, and it was actually a pretty good idea if I had not gotten interrupted.

Nextly, little changeling, you must return to the horde. A goblin is not meant to live so long without its kin and kind. I am surprised you have not withered away and died already—but if you do not return soon, you will certainly die. We all will—every creature of the Wild Wood.

Our last hope lies in a ceremony under the next Veil Moon. If you are not reunited with the horde by then, it will be too late. Magic in

the Wild Wood will die. The horde will die. You
will die. Lots of death.

Follow the goblin trail to the horde at
Hollowcliff at first light tomorrow morning.
Move swiftly. Do not delay. Do not stray from
the path. Do not trust anyone you meet in the
forest. Maybe bring a light snack. Definitely do
not bring any humans you do not wish to see
dead.

From the shadows, Kull breathed deeply. The boys were turning the paper over and giving each other solemn looks. He slipped into the shadows and leaned his back against a tree. It was done. They finally knew what he knew. Well . . . they knew enough of what he knew.

His changeling would come.

SIX

A PAIR OF HAZEL EYES WATCHED THE BOYS climb down from the knotted tree and dash away up the trail. One of the twins was still scrutinizing the paper, while the other glanced back at the tree line every few steps. The eyes kept watching as the little hunched goblin scampered back into the woods, taking practiced steps on mossy ground to muffle his footfalls. For years, those eyes had watched that goblin watch those boys—but something felt different today. Something had shifted. It was in the air. A beam of sunlight found its way down past the canopy of leaves, and the hazel eyes flashed gold for just a moment. Beneath them, a smile grew. Something was beginning.

"It's not real," Cole said as they rounded the last bend in the path. "It's probably just Edgar, from school."

"It feels a little bit real," Tinn said. He turned the letter over for the hundredth time, studying the sketchy little map on the back of the page. "If it *was* real, would you go?"

"Through the Wild Wood?" said Cole. "Past the Oddmire? Beyond the Deep Dark?" He considered. "Maybe. If we were going together, I guess. I think we could do it."

"Even if we made it all the way through the forest, though," Tinn said, "what would happen when we got to the goblin horde? I don't want to be the only human in the middle of a bunch of goblins. The note even said not to bring any humans. Do goblins eat people? Would they eat one of us?"

"I don't think goblins eat people," said Cole. "But, if it *is* real, and if we *don't* go, it sounds like one of us is going to die anyway."

The boys were quiet for a long time.

"It's not real," Cole said, even less convincingly than the first time.

"It feels a little bit real," said Tinn.

When Annie Burton came to tuck her boys into bed, they were already lying under their covers, blankets pulled up to their chins, waiting quietly. Like any good mother, Annie was immediately suspicious.

"Okay. What'd you do?"

"Nothing," they answered together.

"Then what are you planning to do?"

They both hesitated.

"Uh-huh," said Annie. "I don't know about you two, but if I was a boy whose birthday was just around the corner, I would be on my very best behavior in the hopes that my incredibly patient mother would see fit to give me the birthday presents she sent away for three weeks ago and has been hiding ever since they arrived."

"They already came?" said Cole. "Where are they?"

"Nice try, kiddo," said Annie. "They're hidden somewhere you two would never think to look for them."

"Are they in the hatbox in the back of your closet?" said Tinn.

Annie pursed her lips. "By morning they will be hidden somewhere you two would never think to look for them. You best not ruin your birthday! I *will* send your presents back."

"You always say you'll send them back, but you never do," Cole said with a cheeky grin.

"Don't try me."

"Hey, Mom," said Tinn. "How do you know for sure we both have the same birthday?"

Annie took a deep breath. She had resolved, long ago, not to lie to her children. Not outright. If anybody in the village had a right to know their story, it was the two of them—not that there was anybody in the village who *didn't* know their story. "I guess I don't know for sure," she answered. "I was only there for the one of you. Why? You hoping for double birthday cakes?"

"No. Well, now that you mention it, yes. But no."

"What would you do," asked Cole, "if you found out which one of us it is?"

"If I found out which one of you was a goblin?" Annie said.

They both nodded, suddenly intent.

"Hmm. Good question. Can't have a goblin running loose without a plan, can I? What if the mischievous scamp were to get up to some goblin shenanigans, like—I don't know—hiding my good whisk in the icebox and switching my salt and sugar bowls right before I made a batch of marmalade tarts?"

"Okay, that was an accident," said Tinn. "Mostly."

"Right. And what if the naughty troublemaker used my nice tablecloth to turn his climbing tree into a pirate ship?"

"That was Tinn's idea!" said Cole.

"Was not."

"Okay, it was my idea, but Tinn helped."

"I did not!"

"Okay, but he didn't tell me not to, so it's really just as much his fault as it is mine," said Cole. "Also, it made a really good sail, and actually I'm still pretty proud of how it came out. I mean—I'm very sorry and it won't happen again."

"Uh-huh," said Annie Burton. "What would I do if I knew for sure which one of you was a goblin?" She kissed Tinn on the top of his head, then crossed the carpet and kissed Cole. "I would find out what day my little goblin boy was born and bake a special cake just for him. And then I would hide his presents better because apparently an old hatbox in the back of my closet is the very first place you ruffians would look."

"That's where you hid them last year," said Cole.

"You're incorrigible," said Annie.

"What's *incorrigible*?" said Tinn.

"It means go to sleep," said Annie. "As long as you look like my boys and talk like my boys and—God help me—get yourselves into all sorts of trouble like my boys, then you're stuck with me for a mom, and as your mom I say it's time to turn out the lights and go to bed."

"Good night," said Tinn. "I love you."

"I love you, too," said Cole. "'Night."

"Sweet dreams, my little goblin boys," said Annie Burton. "Get plenty of rest, now. You're helping me with the garden tomorrow."

As she clicked the door shut she heard Tinn's voice whisper across the silent bedroom. "Not knowing is the worst part."

"Do you think not knowing is why Dad left?" said Cole.

Annie winced. She hesitated, then leaned her ear closer to the bedroom door.

"Naw. Mom says he never would have left us if he didn't have to."

"But he did leave," said Cole. "He left because of us."

"You don't know that. Maybe he was always gonna come back. Maybe he went looking for answers, like Old Jim says."

"Old Jim doesn't know anything about it. If Dad was planning to come back, would he have left without telling Mom where he was going?"

Tinn shrugged. "Would you wanna tell Mom if you were about to go do something stupid and dangerous?"

Cole considered this. "I would leave a note, at least."

Annie Burton smiled to herself and tiptoed away from their door with a bittersweet sigh. They were good boys, underneath.

"Hey, Tinn?" Cole whispered later that night. "You awake?"

"Yeah," said Tinn.

"Me, too," said Cole. "Are you thinking about the letter?"

"Of course I am," said Tinn.

"Me, too."

They lay in silence for a while as the leaves rustled in the wind outside their window. The letter was tucked inside the top drawer on the nightstand between them. It was only a thin scrap, but in the dark it seemed to take up the entire room. If *not knowing* had been a pebble, then *the possibility of knowing* was a boulder.

"What if it's me?" Cole said at last.

Tinn stared at the ceiling. The letter promised answers to a question both of them had felt pressing the insides of their skulls for as long as either of them could remember.

"I don't want it to be you," whispered Tinn.

Cole sat up and leaned his back against the wall. "What if it's you?"

Tinn lay motionless. He didn't even blink for several seconds.

"I don't want it to be me," he breathed.

Both boys were quiet for a long time. Crickets chirped

rhythmically outside, and a gust of wind rustled the leaves of a big sycamore.

"Hey, Tinn?" Cole whispered again. "If it is me—if I'm a—if you're the real boy and I'm . . . not"—he swallowed—"will you still be my brother?"

Tinn's throat tightened. "Always."

Cole nodded into the dark.

"Hey, Cole," Tinn began.

"Always," said Cole.

Tinn took a deep breath. "We're going to do it, aren't we?" he said.

"Well, if it *is* you, I'm not sitting around to watch you die because we didn't go," said Cole. "I'd rather get eaten in the forest." He swallowed. "You know, *together.*"

Tinn nodded. "Me, too," he said.

"Okay, then," said Cole. "Answers. Wild Wood. Sunrise."

Tinn nodded. The wind whistled against the windowpane. "So, are *you* going to tell Mom?"

Cole bit his lip. "Are you?"

In the morning, Annie Burton found a note.

SEVEN

THE MAP WAS SIMPLE AND CRUDE, BUT THE landmarks inscribed near the forest's edge were familiar enough. The secret path began not far from the tree where the boys had found the message. The morning sun was still hugging the horizon when they arrived at what the map implied was the head of the trail.

Cole had brought with him his pocketknife. It was good and sharp—although not as sharp as it had once been; countless sticks had been whittled to shavings by that blade. He also carried a bundle wrapped in faded yellow cloth. Their mother had indeed made marmalade tarts the night before and left them cooling on the kitchen counter. While Tinn had been carefully writing a note that explained where they were going and telling her not to worry, Cole had stacked a half dozen of the flaky pastries on a faded yellow dish towel and tied the whole thing up in a neat package. He held the bundle in one hand as they trod down the path.

Tinn had swiped a matchbox from the kitchen drawer. It had only four matchsticks left, but he had felt his chances of getting a campfire going were better with four matchsticks than with none. With each step, the box rattled faintly in his trouser pocket. Tinn also held the map.

"If this thing is real," he said as they passed the knotty oak and stepped over the tall grass toward the tree line, "then there's a path somewhere just on the other side of the stream."

"Well?" said Cole. "Let's find out."

They jumped the stream together and pressed into the foliage on the other side.

A tingle went up Cole's spine. He grinned. "We're in the Wild Wood," he whispered. "Uncharted territory."

"It's not uncharted," Tinn whispered back. "We're twenty feet from where we hang out every day, and I am literally holding a chart."

"Don't ruin this. You see a trail yet?"

Tinn gazed around at the trees and mossy rocks and

wildflowers. There were a lot of things in the forest that were not a path. For just a moment he entertained the notion that there was no path—that the letter had been fake all along. Of course, there was no secret trail, no imminent danger, no goblin horde. He was just beginning to look forward to a blissful morning of eating marmalade tarts in the safety of their climbing tree when his feet slid out from under him on a patch of dewy moss, sending him half falling, half hopping through a curtain of branches. His heart jumped as he regained his footing and looked around.

"Whoa," said Cole, joining him.

Before them stretched a long, winding trail. It was a thin strip carpeted with needles and leaves, tall grasses and shrubs pressing in on it from either side. Unlike the straight, neat paths in town, this one wove in and out along the forest floor, skirting roots and boulders in a wavy zigzag.

"It looks like an animal path," said Cole. "Maybe deer?"

"Maybe." Tinn glanced back down at the paper in his hands. "It's in the right place for a goblin trail, though."

Cole's whole body tingled. He looked at Tinn.

Tinn felt slightly numb. He nodded to Cole.

Frankly, Cole thought as the sun climbed higher and higher in the sky, he had expected the mysterious goblin trail to be slightly more mysterious and decidedly more goblin-y. It had been hours, and there had been no sign of eldritch talismans hung from tree branches or strange statues half buried in the ground to mark their way.

They had followed the meandering forest path for miles as it climbed quiet hills, dipped through shady valleys, and crossed burbling creeks. The path grew so thin in places they had lost it once or twice, but with the help of the map, they had managed to pick it up again each time. Cole used his pocketknife to carve a jagged C into the bark of nearby trees from time to time, in case they got lost and had to find their way back—and also because it helped to break up the plodding journey.

The Wild Wood was not as wild as its name implied, but it was certainly alive. There was a steady buzz of insects and a clamor of birds, chirping and cawing incessantly. The boys caught sight of a doe in a thicket, although it bolted the moment it heard them coming, and Cole spotted a family of squirrels racing along the branches. Tinn paused at a tree raked with claw marks.

"You think there are mountain lions out here?" he asked.

"I don't think so," said Cole. "There aren't any *mountains* out here. More like *hill* lions, maybe? I'm hungry. Are you hungry?"

"I bet there are," said Tinn. "Cougars and wolves and all sorts of things." His chest felt tight. Was it his imagination, or was the air thicker in this part of the forest? He hadn't noticed it before, but a fine mist was drifting between the trees, winding and twisting around their roots. He peered at the map again until he found a scribble that bore a passing resemblance to the boulder up ahead. If he was right, then the Oddmire was very close. The goblin crossing would be nearby.

"Let's take a break," Cole said. "It's basically lunchtime. You want a tart?" He sat down on a mossy log and began to fiddle with the knot in his dish-towel bundle.

"Hold on. Do you hear something?" Tinn said. He strained his ears. He could have sworn he heard a voice.

Cole paused to listen. In the distance there was a quiet splashing and a piteous mewling. "Is that a person or an animal?"

The boys traded a wary glance. Cole pushed himself up. Neither one of them spoke as they stepped off the goblin path.

The fog grew thicker with each step they took, and the ground grew softer. They followed the sound of the wailing farther into the forest until the trees opened onto a wide, marshy swamp.

"I guess we found the Oddmire," Tinn said. "Whew, that's a stink. It smells like armpits and wet possum."

"Look!" Cole pointed. Ten feet out, an animal was struggling to keep its head above the muck. It was not a large creature. It was brown or black from the look of it, although it was hard to tell with the slime of the mire all over it. The beast's desperate cries increased at the sight of the boys.

Cole took a step closer and immediately sank one leg up to his ankle in swampy peat. He pulled back with a wet sucking sound. "How did that critter even get out so far?"

The thick roots of a tree beside them wound into the muck like a heavy rope, weaving in and out until it reached a small, damp island, just a few feet away from the trapped creature.

"Along here," Tinn said. He tucked the map into his pocket and took slow steps out along the slimy roots, balancing as best he could above the stagnant water until he was as close as he could get to the pitiful creature. "I think it's a cub," he called back to Cole. "A bear cub. I'll see if I can grab it."

"Careful!" Cole called. The cub redoubled its efforts as Tinn reached for it, but he was too far away, and the cub's thrashing only churned up the slime, nearly sending it under.

"I can't reach it," said Tinn.

Cole looked around until he found a sturdy fallen branch. It was soft with rot, but at least it was thick and didn't crumble to pieces when he banged it experimentally against a tree trunk. "Here, try this!" He edged out after his brother, treading unsteadily onto the roots, which sank farther under their combined weight until both boys' boots were completely buried. When he was within reach, Cole passed the branch to Tinn.

Tinn eased it toward the frightened cub. The little bear pawed desperately at the branch a few times before catching hold, and then eagerly sank its claws into the wood and pulled. Tinn was nearly hauled face-first into the mire, but Cole caught his hand. Together they pulled the cub back to shore, inch by grueling inch, the thick stew of peat and plants and filthy water tugging back at them every step of the way.

When they had finally deposited the bear cub on solid ground, it shook itself like a wet dog, spraying the grass and the trees and the boys and everything else in a ten-foot radius with slime and mud before collapsing.

Tinn chuckled and wiped the mess from his face. "You're welcome," he told the cub.

Cole traded his dish-towel bundle from one hand to the other as he wiped his palms off on his shirt. His pant legs were soaked up to the knees. "I guess no good deed goes un—" He froze. The color drained from his face.

"What?" Tinn turned around in time to watch the broad, dark shadow behind him rise up on two muscular, hairy legs. It was a mountain of heavy brown fur with a jet-black nose. Black lips peeled back over the long, sharp fangs of the most enormous animal the twins had ever seen.

For a moment, neither of them dared so much as blink. The bear looked down at the damp, motionless cub lying in a heap between the two boys, and then its furry chest swelled as it drew a long breath.

It roared.

The bear bellowed a deep, booming, bone-rattling roar that Tinn and Cole felt in the pits of their stomachs. The noise echoed inside them, rattling those nerves typically reserved for falling blindly backward or waking from a nightmare. The boys did not fall over backward or wake from anything.

The boys ran.

EIGHT

ANNIE BURTON AWOKE WITH THE SUNLIGHT climbing over her windowsill. She rubbed her eyes and stretched. The house was quiet. Her stockinged feet padded past the boys' room. They could sleep in. They had promised to help her clear the last of the blackberry vines from the back garden days ago, but she would enjoy her tea first, and then rouse them with a healthy breakfast before putting them to work.

She filled the copper kettle and tucked a couple of slim, dry logs into the potbellied stove. She reached into the drawer for her matches, but the box was gone. Her eyes searched the countertop and noticed the much diminished pile of marmalade tarts—those rotten rascals!

"Boys!" she yelled down the hallway. "I *know* you didn't help yourself to my tarts last night! I know I didn't raise a pair of sneaky little thieves who don't respect—" She stormed into their bedroom. It contained a decided absence of boys. She gritted her teeth.

"Boys!" she hollered from the front door. "BOYS!"

"They up to their mischief already this morning, Annie?" called Mrs. Grouse from across the way, sloshing her watering can on her slippers. "That's half an hour earlier than yesterday."

"Never mind, Helen." Annie ducked back inside. Those boys owed her so much more than weeding. As soon as she caught up with them . . .

She leaned on the counter with both hands and sighed through her teeth. Just one day. Just one *morning*. Was it too much to ask for a single hot cup of tea before those little devils got started?

There were tart crumbs all over the countertop. And a note. She straightened. She picked up the little paper and read it. It was Tinn's handwriting—always just a little neater than Cole's—but he had signed for both of them. She read it again.

Annie Burton put on her boots.

Annie Burton did not make tea.

59

NINE

Cole's lungs felt like they were going to burst. He and Tinn had run as fast as they could through leaves and hanging vines, vaulting over rocks and fallen trees until they could no longer hear the bear's huge claws raking through the bark and slicing branches behind them—and then they had run farther still.

Tinn sank, panting, against the foot of a pine tree. Cole flopped flat on his back on the cold earth in the middle of the clearing. For several minutes they just breathed.

"Well . . . it . . . wasn't . . ." Cole huffed, "a . . . mountain lion."

Tinn shook his head and threw a pinecone at his

brother. Cole chuckled in spite of himself. Tinn could feel his heartbeat beginning to calm.

After several minutes, Cole let out a wistful sigh. "I just wish I hadn't let go of those tarts," he said.

"It's not your fault. You had more important— Wait. No." Tinn reached into his pockets. He pulled out the matchbox and a handful of lint. "Oh, no." He turned out all of his pockets and pushed himself up from the pine needles, looking all around him. "Oh, no, no, no!"

"What? What is it?" Cole pushed himself up, too.

"The map!" Tinn wailed, thudding his head against the trunk of the tree. "It's gone!"

He collapsed again beneath the tree. "It must've fallen out of my pocket while we were running." He could feel tears welling, but he forced them back. He hung his head so that Cole couldn't see his eyes.

"Hey, it's okay," said Cole. "We just—we'll have to find our own way, that's all. There's a path across the Oddmire, right? We can find that." His stomach gurgled audibly.

"And something to eat?" said Tinn.

"We can find food, too. People used to find food in the forest all the time, like mushrooms and nuts and things. There were some cattails back by the marsh—I think I heard that you can eat those. Hey, look! Right there. I think those might be huckleberries." Cole crossed the clearing

61

and plucked a deep purple berry from a low bush. "Yeah. Huckleberries." He sniffed it experimentally. "I'm pretty sure."

Before he could pop one of the plump berries into his mouth, a voice called out from behind them, "You probably shouldn't eat those ones."

Both boys spun around. A girl with bright hazel eyes was seated on a thick branch ten or fifteen feet above them. She looked about their age, if a little smaller. Her hair was a mess of curly, knotted strands, hung with twigs and leaves, and her dress was little more than a canvas sack with a bit of style. It appeared to have been dyed in ink made of only the finest dirt.

"Those ones make you fart and barf a lot and maybe die," she added, kicking her feet absently as she took a bite of a flaky tart.

"Where did you come from?" asked Tinn.

"Wait a second," Cole said. "Where did you get that? Those are ours!"

"I know. You dropped them. They're super good." She stuffed the rest of the tart in her mouth. "Forry! No more left!"

"Have you been watching us?" Tinn asked.

"Mm-hmm." She nodded, crumbs dribbling down her chin. "For a really long time."

"Well, stop it," said Tinn. "You shouldn't be out this far, anyway."

"We're on a really dangerous quest," Cole added with a somber nod. "We're going beyond the Deep Dark Forest to find the goblin horde."

"Ooh! Fun! I'll come with you!" the girl cried, her face alight. She swung herself backward off the branch, caught another on the way down, and then landed smoothly on her feet.

"What? No," said Tinn. "We're not taking you with us."

"Why not? You need to find the goblin horn. I know where that is!"

Tinn glanced at his brother. Cole shrugged.

"You mean the goblin *horde*?" asked Tinn.

"Yes! That thing. I know all about that thing! These are my woods. They're in my blood."

Cole looked skeptically at the girl. "You certainly have enough of them in your hair," he said, although Tinn could detect a glimmer of admiration in his comment.

The girl just looked back and forth hopefully between the two boys.

"Give us a moment, would you?" Tinn leaned into his brother. "We can't seriously be thinking about taking her with us," he whispered. "We don't know anything about her. We don't even know her name."

"Fable," whispered the girl. Tinn started and spun around. She had slipped next to the boys without making a sound. "My name," she said. "It's Fable." She stared at Tinn for several seconds and then smiled broadly. "It's a *people* name."

Tinn took a step back. "Okay. Yes. Fable. Hi."

"Where did you come from?" asked Cole.

Fable crinkled her eyebrows. "From here," she said.

"Well, sure—but what town?" Cole persisted. "I mean, you must have come from somewhere. You speak English, and you're wearing clothes and everything, so it's not like you were raised by wolves in the forest. Did you run away from home or something?"

"I am home," Fable said. "What's English?"

Tinn shook his head. "It's what you're speaking!"

"Oh." Fable scrunched up her nose. "I call these words. These are people words."

"Yeah, they're words," said Tinn. "But people speak lots of different languages. English words aren't the only kind of words."

"Oh!" Fable looked intrigued. "What other languages do you speak?"

"I—well, I don't. I mean . . . I just speak English, but people speak loads of different languages."

Fable's eyebrows knit together again. "Oh. I thought you were people."

"What?" Tinn was beginning to have trouble keeping up. "Of course we're people!"

"I think you're a little confused about this whole words thing, then," Fable declared. She continued to survey the twins with interest.

"We're not the ones who're confused!" Tinn said.

"There are lots of different kinds of people from lots of different places and not all of them speak English," Cole said. "Don't you know anything about anything?"

"I know how to get to the goblin horde," Fable answered. "Do you?"

Cole and Tinn fell silent. They exchanged glances.

"That's what I thought," Fable said, grinning. "See? I know things. It's settled, then. We're going to have an adventure together! And then we're going to be best friends forever and ever and ever, I know it." She hopped off into the forest, bounding from grass to rocks to fallen trees. "Come on!"

"Well," Cole sighed. "She does have a point."

"I really don't know about her," Tinn said.

"I know we don't have much time," said Cole. "One of us is probably going to die, and maybe a lot of other people, too, unless we make it to that horde—and there's an awful lot of forest that I *don't* want to see before we get there."

The bushes behind the boys rustled, and they both jumped. Beyond the foliage something large was pressing toward them through the branches, huffing and chuffing as it moved.

"Are you two coming?" Fable yelled from the opposite direction.

Tinn swallowed. He glanced from his brother to the bushes behind them to the forest up ahead. Cole took a deep breath and jumped up onto a fallen tree after Fable. "We're coming," he said.

The thing beyond the leaves was growing louder as it neared, and Tinn did not have any desire to greet it alone when it emerged. He vaulted up after his brother, and together they hurried to follow the strange girl into the strange woods.

TEN

ANNIE BURTON BRUSHED A HAND ALONG THE
knotty trunk of her boys' climbing tree. She panted. She
had been hanging on to the tenuous hope that the boys
would be here, playing pirates or just hanging upside down
from the branches. Tinn's note had said that they would
be taking a secret path all the way from their tree to the
far side of the Deep Dark, and not to worry over them,
and also not to be too cross about them stealing the tarts,
which, he had added, was Cole's idea.

Annie tried to slow her breathing. A lesser mother
might have been panicking just then. A mother whose
nerves had not been tested by two puckish little boys

67

for nearly thirteen years might have been a mess of anxious energy and nerves. Annie Burton gritted her teeth. Her boys did not need a lesser mother right now. They needed her.

She scanned the area and spotted muddy footprints on the far side of the creek. Bingo. She took a deep breath. Once they were safe she could fall to pieces and rant and holler and ground them for a million years. Until then, Annie Burton was going to be strong, she was going to be tough, and she was going into the Wild Wood.

ELEVEN

"HOLD ON A MINUTE. I NEED TO USE THE LAVA-tory," said Tinn.

"What's a lavatory?" said Fable.

"A bathroom?" said Tinn.

Fable looked at him blankly.

"Oh, never mind. I'm going to go behind this tree. Wait for me for just a second."

Tinn stepped behind a thick pine. Fable peeked her head around the other side. "Okay. What's a bathroom?"

"Oh! For goodness' sake. I need to . . . you know . . . *go*." He nodded downward.

"But we said we would go together."

"PEE! I need to pee!"

"Oh. Why are you hiding? I don't mind. I pee. Everybody pees."

"Well, I do mind. I don't want to pee in front of someone."

"I bet your brother doesn't mind, either. Aren't you exactly the same, anyway? It isn't like he hasn't seen what you look like underneath. Can I see what you look like underneath?"

"Ack! No! Go away!"

Fable shrugged and walked back to Cole.

"Your brother is weird."

Cole shrugged. "We've been called a lot worse."

"What do people call you?"

"Well, goblins, mostly."

"Why do people call you goblins?"

"Because we are, I guess. Or one of us is. That's the story, anyway. That's why we need to get to the other side of the forest and find the goblin horde. One of us is a . . . well, a changeling." It felt strange to say it out loud so matter-of-factly. He had never had to tell anyone in town the story. They all already knew as much as he did. He spent more time awkwardly avoiding talking about it because of how uncomfortable it made most of the other kids.

"That's neat. Which one of you is it?" asked Fable.

"We don't know," said Cole. "We just know it's one of us."

"How can you not know what you are on the inside?"

"I don't know. How does anybody know what they are? One of us is a human and one of us is a goblin. That's all we know."

Fable considered this. "Maybe you're both half-goblin and half-human. Then you're exactly one person and one goblin put together."

"No, it doesn't work like that."

"Yes it does. It's called math. A half and a half and a half and a half make two."

"I know what math is. That's just not how being a person works. Either you're a person or you're not."

"That's silly. I'm lots of things at the same time. Sometimes I'm tired and excited and hungry all at once."

"That's different. That's feelings."

Fable leaned against a log. "So, what does being a goblin *feel* like?"

Cole took a deep breath. "I don't know. I think maybe it feels like . . ." He trailed off.

"Do *you* feel like a goblin?"

"Sometimes?" Cole sighed. "I don't know!"

Fable watched his expression with interest.

"It's like this," Cole tried. "I don't mean to be trouble.

It's not like I do it on purpose. Not usually. I mean—sometimes." He felt his ears get hot as the words tumbled clumsily in his mouth. "Sometimes I get an idea, and it feels like a really good idea at the time, and so I just do it. I don't even feel like I'm doing something bad until it's too late. But it *is* a bad idea. It's pretty much always a bad idea. And afterward I know it was a bad idea, but I still did it, and I'll still do it again the next time, too. And worse, when I've already messed up, I almost always know what I *should* do to make things better, but I get another bad idea instead, and I just do that. I don't mean to screw everything up. I just—it's like there's something inside me that wants to make everything . . . I don't know . . . bad."

Fable nodded sagely. "So, is that a goblin feeling, or a person feeling?"

"I don't know." Cole slumped down on the log beside her. "I worry sometimes that it is the goblin. I don't want to be the changeling. I don't want my mom to not really be my mom." He rubbed the back of his neck and stared at his muddy shoes. "But, other times . . ."

"Other times what?"

"Other times I don't worry. Other times I wish."

"You wish you *were* a goblin?"

"Sort of? A little? Ugh. I mean—goblins are *supposed* to cause all kinds of mischief and run around having crazy adventures, you know? Maybe being the changeling would be kind of okay."

"But you already make mischief as a human boy. Why would being a goblin be different?"

"Well, if I was a goblin, maybe I wouldn't have to feel bad about it."

"Goblins don't feel bad about stuff?"

"I don't know! Argh! All I know is that people who *might* be goblins feel bad about stuff all the time! That's why I think it might just be better for everybody if I wasn't a real boy." He sagged. "That—and the other thing."

"What's the other thing?"

Cole glanced at the pine tree. He lowered his voice. "If *I'm* the one who doesn't belong," he said, "if *I'm* the goblin child—then Tinn doesn't have to be. I don't want to go live in some wild goblin horde, not really. Not even when I'm feeling especially wicked. I don't want to lose my mom and my brother. But Tinn . . . I could never do that to him. He's not as strong as me."

"I thought you were exactly the same."

"Only on the outside. On the inside . . ." Cole sighed again, trying to find the words. "Tinn's special. He's just—he's a better person than I am. If all the worst stuff we do is because of me, then all the best stuff we do is because of Tinn. He's . . . good, deep down. Even when I'm terrible, he never leaves me to get in trouble alone. He's always fixing my mistakes. If I could only do one worthy thing in my whole life, it would be letting Tinn be the real boy."

Fable nodded, but her brows furrowed. "I can't tell. Are you more worried that you *are* a goblin or more worried that you're *not*?"

Cole sighed again. "Yes?" he said.

Fable looked like she would like to say more, but Tinn was finally coming out from behind the tree, and Cole shot her a stern glance before standing up.

"Took you long enough," Cole jibed.

"You know I can't pee when it feels like someone's watching," said Tinn. "She made me all nervous. What were you two talking about?"

"Nobody was watching," said Cole.

"I was kinda watching," said Fable. "But you made it really hard to see what you were doing and that tree was right in the way. Do you pee standing up? People pee smells funny."

"Shut up! You can't smell my pee from way over there."

"I'm a really good smeller."

"Come on," said Cole. "We should get moving. I don't want to be out here when the sun goes down."

TWELVE

Kull waited. he sat with infinite patience on the soggy log, waggled his calloused green toes, drummed his fingernails on the mossy wood. He waited. Gradually, his patience became somewhat less infinite. In fact, it began to grow decidedly finite.

He was tucked out of sight of any accidental observer, unless they were to march directly up the ancient path— and even then they would need to be nearly on top of him before he would be spotted. There was no way to stumble upon the hidden bridge unless you were goblin-born. There was magic involved, yes, but it was much more elegant than that. The goblin ward was nothing more than a subtle nudge. The real artistry was in the angles. However one approached the bridge, every instinct pulled a traveler away. Seeking good fortune? The clearings to either side looked much more promising. Avoiding trouble? The path that led to the bridge looked trickiest and wildest. Seeking to explore the unknown? There appeared to be nothing down this route but mist and mire and a dull, dead end.

Kull waited.

His changeling would come. The wee goblin child had worn those human eyes for so long, he might not even remember how to be a goblin—but underneath his glamour, a goblin was still a goblin. He was still kin. He had to feel the pull. This path was still his heritage. It would call to him. And, of course, failing all that, he had the map that Kull had drawn.

Yes, he would meet the child here, where Chief Nudd could hardly accuse Kull of crossing into human lands, and then he would march the changeling back into the horde with his head held high. Finally, after all these years, they would be happy to see him.

Kull waited.

Annie Burton ran along the forest path. It had not been hard to follow the thick, muddy footprints from the creek

up to the narrow trail. The jagged C carvings she continued to spot in the tree trunks along the path reassured her
that Cole had definitely been this way—and wherever Cole
had gone, Tinn had surely followed.

More than once, the path faded, erased by the encroach-
ing forest, but she was able to find signs of the boys again
each time. Now and then she would hear a sudden flutter
of wing beats or a roar in the distance, and each sound
made her heart skip.

After she had been searching for what must have been
hours, the footprints seemed to veer off the forest path.
Annie pressed through the underbrush until she saw a
wide, misty swamp stretching out before her. Surely her
boys knew better than to go anywhere near the Oddmire.
Her eyes continued scanning the ground for trampled grass
or broken twigs or—marmalade? At the foot of a sticky log
lay her crumpled yellow dish towel. Annie snatched it up.
It was muddy and covered in crumbs and sticky orange
jam. She peered around. The ground was a mess of recent
impressions: familiar shoe prints overlapped with the marks
of enormous paws.

The forest spun around her and she took slow breaths.
She tried to see where the prints led, but they all seemed to
double over themselves in a meaningless knot. Finally, she
spotted a paper, caught in the branches of a little bush. Its

edges were flapping in the faint breeze that came rolling off the mire.

She picked it up and unfolded it. On one side was a note. It began, *Once upon a time* . . . On the other side was a crudely drawn map.

The changeling should have come along hours since. Kull had promised Chief Nudd he would not go to the boy, promised him on his goblin heart that he would not steal, summon, or even speak to the children as long as they remained within the safety of the human town. Goblin promises are more powerful than human ones. It had only been through Kull's painstakingly creative interpretation of his own oath that he had found it possible to come so close. If the boy came to him, well, then there was no promise broken.

Time was no longer *running* out—it *was* out. Kull jumped down from the damp log. He was just going to have to . . .

Footsteps thudded through the bracken ahead.

Kull's ears perked up. He was here! After thirteen miserable years, something in Kull's wretched life was finally going to go right. He stood up straighter, adjusting his manky, matted vest. He put his hands behind his back, then held them at his sides instead. He considered leaning nonchalantly against the log, then decided against it. Deep breath. This was it.

At last, the arrival exploded through the leaves, a tattered goblin map clutched in her hands.

Kull stared at the woman, who stared back at Kull.

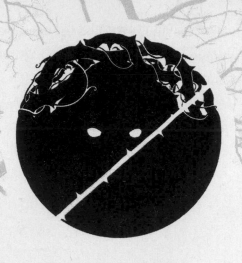

THIRTEEN

THICK BLACK VINES QUIVERED LIKE THE strands of a spiderweb. There were footsteps moving through the forest. Deep within the inky darkness, in the center of a mountain of thorns, the Thing awoke. It sniffed the air.

Beyond its shadowy home, beyond the stench of dust and rot and dry bones, beyond the chill winds of the Deep Dark Forest, the Thing smelled fear. There were flies moving across its web. It could feel them. It could taste them.

The forest around it was dying. The Thing knew it. It could feel death seeping in. There were so few beings left to call the woods their home, fewer still with any real magic. The Thing had gotten greedy and careless. It had killed too many, eaten too deeply. It had starved itself with its own gluttony, and now the meals came so few and far between.

The Thing was starting to remember old feelings now, feelings it thought it had buried long ago with its own true shadow. For the first time in years, it felt empty and cold. And small. It had been so long since the Thing had allowed itself to feel small. It did not know if it was strong enough to be small again. It did not wish to find out.

No. The Thing was never going back. In the heart of that dying forest, the Thing drew the shadows around itself, growing larger and larger, until it stood as tall as it had on its first night, still cloaked in its tattered shroud of darkness.

As the forest died, so too the Thing would die. It had accepted this fate. But before it died, it would feed one last time. It would gorge. It would suck the marrow from the bone.

FOURTEEN

"WAIT UP," SAID TINN, PULLING HIS FOOT FREE of a particularly persistent, stringy root. "We've been walking for ages. Are you sure you're not lost?"

Fable made a face. "I keep telling you, this is my forest. Mine and my mama's. I know exactly where I am."

"Hey!" called Cole from a little way up the next hill. "There's a building over here! Beneath the vines!"

"You found it!" Fable clapped. "I was wondering if you'd notice."

"It's a whole cottage! It's got a front door and everything." Cole peeled back the greenery, layer by layer. "Is this your mother's house?"

"No," said Fable. "My mother doesn't like to come here. It makes her sad."

Tinn slowed, giving the cottage a wide berth as his brother picked his way around it, tugging at ivy and peering in through the cracks. "Why should this old house make your mother sad?" Tinn asked.

"It reminds her that she was too late," Fable answered.

"Too late for what?"

She shrugged. "I don't know. She won't tell me that part. She always gets sorta quiet and then remembers something important we really need to do somewhere else."

Tinn swallowed, glancing around at the mossy trees that encircled the hovel. "I don't like it."

Fable stared at Tinn. The boy looked identical to his brother, down to the last freckle. Really looking at them, it was easy to believe that one of them was a magical copy of the other. Cole had seemed nervous to speak openly about the changeling thing. If she was going to bring it up with Tinn, she would need—what was the people word?—*tact*. Fable had learned all about tact. Tact was the thing that people did to make their words behave. Tact kept other people from feeling bad because of the things you said. Fable pursed her lips as she considered how to bring up the matter tactfully.

"Why are you staring at me?" said Tinn. "Stop it."

"Are you a goblin?" said Fable. Tact was hard. "Sorry," she said. "But are you?"

Tinn shrugged. "I don't know." That question had haunted him his whole life. After all these years, if they ever reached the goblin horde, this might be the last time that he did not have an answer. He felt a lump in his throat as he thought about it. One way or another, at the end of this, one human boy would leave the forest, and one goblin would stay behind. They would have the final terrible answer to their terrible question.

Cole was picking his way around the back of the cottage now.

"Be careful!" Tinn called. Cole waved him away as he slipped around the corner.

"Do you *feel* like a goblin?" Fable asked.

Tinn swallowed. "Sometimes, I guess? Why are you asking me about this?"

"Sometimes *how*?"

"I don't know! Just, sometimes—I just worry, I guess. I worry that I'm not my own person."

"Then whose person are you?"

"It's hard to explain. Everyone else seems to know what they want and what will make them happy all the time— but I have no idea. Ordinary people get offered choices and they just pick one without needing to see what somebody else picked. I never know what I want. Cole makes choices all the time. Stupid choices, fun choices." He kicked at the moss. "I never imagined going out into the Wild Wood, but you know what? None of it scares me half as much as just being alone in a room all by myself."

"Why?" said Fable. "What's it like when you're all alone?"

"I don't know! I've never had to be alone. I've always had Cole and he's always had me. I don't know who I'd be without him. I don't want to know. That's what's so scary. I don't think ordinary people think like that. I don't think ordinary people are afraid of figuring out who they are on the inside. I don't think I am ordinary. I worry about it a lot, actually. And the more I worry about it, the more I worry that I'm right to worry."

"Dang. You *really* don't want to be the changeling, do you?"

"I really don't," said Tinn, "most of the time. But other times . . ."

"Other times, what?"

"Other times, I hope it is me. Don't tell Cole. Sometimes I hope I am the changeling, because I wouldn't want Cole to leave me and go off to live with the goblins without me. I don't want to be left alone. If I was the changeling, maybe then I would forget all about being a person when I changed back into a goblin, and then I wouldn't have to be afraid of everything anymore."

"Goblins aren't afraid of stuff?"

"I don't know." Tinn took a deep breath. "They're probably afraid of different stuff. And there's another reason, too."

Fable waited patiently.

"Cole's just better at living—better at being a person—than I am. He's a good person."

"How?"

"Lots of ways. Like one time, these kids in school were picking on my friend Evie, just because she's small. They did it for weeks and I didn't do anything. I didn't know what to do. I hated those kids. Cole found out and he just fixed it. Right then."

"Did he hurt them?"

"Not exactly. He had a bunch of marbles tied up in a handkerchief, so he poured them out into his pocket and handed the handkerchief to Evie, who just looked at him funny. Then he loaded up his fountain pen in the ink well and sprayed ink all over one of the bullies. Right in the guy's face. Everybody laughed at him. I laughed at him. Evie wound up being the only one to help the guy get cleaned up. She already had the handkerchief in her hands. Then Cole tripped one of the worst girls in our class so she fell into a big mud puddle right in front of Evie. Everybody laughed again, except Evie. Evie helped pick her up and get her dried off. Cole planned a whole day full of terrible, awful, wicked ways to mess with those bullies, and I helped. It felt good. That probably sounds rotten, but it did. In the end, they hated us more than anything, but they stopped being mean to Evie. Cole did that. In one afternoon."

Tinn looked down at his feet. "Cole can't be the changeling." He fidgeted with his shirt and avoided Fable's scrutinizing gaze. "If I could manage to do one worthwhile thing in my whole life, it would be to let Cole be the real boy. He'd be loads better at it, anyway."

Fable watched him fidget with the hem of his shirt for a few seconds before she spoke. "Are you more worried that you *are* a goblin or more worried that you're *not*?"

Tinn shrugged again, miserably. "Yes?"

"That," said Fable, "is super unhelpful."

Cole had come back around to what appeared to be the front door of the cottage. He pushed a final handful of leaves aside and tapped on the dusty glass windowpane.

"Careful," Tinn called to him. "This place might belong to the witch."

"If it does, she sure hasn't used it in a long time," said Cole. Thick moss blanketed the windowsill and shutters, and he could see spiderwebs crisscrossing the room and tall weeds growing through the floorboards in one corner. He let the vines fall back over the window.

"Nobody has used it in ages," agreed Fable. "Except there was a family of raccoons who lived in it for a little while. What's a witch?"

"What's a witch?" echoed Tinn.

"The Witch of the Wood?" Cole said, stepping back toward them over the roots that had overtaken the front walk. "Queen of the Deep Dark? Mother of Monsters? She blights crops and eats children?"

Fable made a face. "What's she do that for? Wouldn't it make more sense to blight the children and eat the crops?"

"Never mind." Cole clambered down from the hill, brushing his hands on his pants. "It's just an old house," he said.

"But what it's not is a bridge over a swamp," said Tinn. "Are you sure this is the right way to get to the goblin horde?"

"Yes. Absolutely," Fable said with a firm nod. "I'm almost positive. Just to be sure, though, goblins are the sort of greenish ones, right? And also, what is a horde, exactly? Oh! And also, do you like blueberries? Blueberries are my favorite."

"What? What do you mean?" Tinn felt his whole face turning red. "No, no, no, no!"

"Calm down! It's just blueberries."

"You have no idea where we are, do you?" Tinn yelled.

"Of course I do. We're in the Wild Wood, stupid. My woods."

"Argh! We're way too far north! I knew we shouldn't have listened to her. We should've crossed the Oddmire ages ago."

"You wanna cross the Oddmire?" Fable asked, raising a dusty eyebrow.

"I—what—but you said . . ." Tinn sputtered. "YES! That's what we've been—argh! Yes, we need to cross the Oddmire!"

"Have you ever tried before? I have. I'm an expert at trying to cross the Oddmire. I've tried forty-seven times. I got pretty far once, but I think I got a little turned around, because I accidentally wound up back on this side in the end. The Oddmire flips the whole forward-and-backward thing around sometimes. Anyway, I'm bound to get across it next time. You should come with me so you can be there when I finally do!"

Tinn's mouth hung open for several seconds.

"You've never been to the other side of the mire?" said Cole.

"I can't believe this!" Tinn fumed, spinning around and marching back the way they had come. "I knew we shouldn't have trusted her!"

Cole gave the girl a sour look before launching after his brother.

"Wait for me!" called Fable behind them.

Tinn ignored her, pressing through knee-high foliage, smacking the stubborn shrubbery down with a branch—as much to clear a path as to vent his frustration. Cole kept close behind, following in his brother's wake of trampled ferns and mangled leaves.

Tinn's angry progress was too noisy for any of them to hear the low growl that rumbled through the forest. Somewhere deep in the Wild Wood, claws churned the earth and a wet black nose sniffed the air. The great lumbering bear had one thought in its head.

It would find the children, and it would not rest until it did.

FIFTEEN

"Yer na my changelin'," Kull managed after he and Annie had exchanged a long and awkward silence.

"You're a—" Annie stammered. "You're a—"

"A goblin?" prompted Kull.

"A goblin." Annie found her composure. She took a deep breath and immediately lost it again. "You're a goblin! You're *the* goblin, aren't you? The one who—did you write this?" She brandished the creased and tattered paper for Kull to see.

"Name's Kull," he said.

"I don't care what your name is! And if you think I'm about to politely introduce myself, like we were meeting at some friendly church potluck, then—"

"Yer name's Annie Burton," said Kull.

Annie faltered. "How," she said with measured breaths, "do you know my name?"

"Been spyin' on yer kids for nigh on thirteen years, haven't I? Bound ta pick up a wee bit. Know a lot more'n yer name."

Annie blinked.

"New boots?" Kull asked.

"WHERE ARE MY CHILDREN?"

"Otch! Ya dinna have ta holler. I'm just as keen ta know where the blighted boys are as ya are. Maybe more keen."

Annie's eye twitched.

"No sense gettin' angry at me, womern. We's both ta blame fer the whole thing, really."

"Both to blame?" Annie managed through clenched teeth. "You think so?"

"Aye. Iffin ya had just stayed asleep when I was makin' the switch, I wouldn'a have had ta rush the job. If ya hadn'a interrupted me, I ne'er would've left without . . . er . . . hmm . . ." He trailed off, glancing up at Annie, whose face was going quite red.

"Go ahead, goblin. Finish your sentence."

"Ah. Doesn'a matter." Kull cleared his throat. "Point is, there's fault here an' fault there, but gettin' the changelin' back—that's what's important."

"No, no. I think it might matter a little, actually," Annie pressed. "You never would have left without what? What could you have possibly been about to say?"

Kull mumbled something and inspected his toes.

"Maybe you were going to say that if I had not interrupted you while you were trespassing in my house, then you would never have left without kidnapping my son and stealing him into the forest to be lost to me forever. Is that about right?"

"Maybe somethin' along those lines. Aye, but everythin' sounds awful when ya say it out loud like that."

"You tried to steal my baby!"

"An' I said I was sorry!"

"No, actually. Not that it much matters, but you didn't!"

"Well, maybe I would have said sorry, iffin ya weren't yellin' at me about every little mistake that happened years ago!"

"Every little—" Annie gritted her teeth and pinched the bridge of her nose with one hand. "You tried to steal my baby, and you're literally *still* trying to steal my baby!"

"I am na! Keep yer blasted boy! I'm tryin' ta steal mine back! Been tryin' ta get the wee changelin' back since the day I left him. I canna seem ta sort out which is which, though—an' I been bound by oath na ta mess with yorn again. See, none o' this is how it was supposed ta go. Twins? Brothers? Bah! The pair of them was ne'er meant ta know one another at all! A changelin' is only supposed ta see its human fer a moment. The goblin imprints, then the human is—erm—taken. With na baby ta mimic, goblin goes back ta bein' a goblin soon enough, finds his way home ta the horde, an' the whole thing's done and over with inside a week. Except I had ta go an' mess everythin' up."

"I see messing up is something you've kept consistent over the last thirteen years. You swore an oath not to mess with my boys? Well, thanks to your rotten message, both of them are now lost in these horrible woods!"

Annie's voice caught in her throat on the last words, and she found a well of fear waiting just behind her anger.

Kull watched in uncomfortable silence for several seconds as her shoulders rose and fell. "The forest isn'a so bad," he offered, gamely. "Well—I suppose there are wolves an' bears an' great big snakes," he mused.

Annie shot him a poisonous glare.

"But there's na any proper monsters!" he added hastily. "Well—na on *this* end o' the forest, anyway." He paused. "Well—"

"If you say *well* one more time," Annie growled, "then I swear to you *I* will become the scariest thing in the Wild Wood." She took a deep breath. "I don't know why we're even still standing here. I'm going to go find my boys."

Annie spun on her heel and stormed back into the bracken.

"I am, though," came a voice at her heels a few minutes later.

"You are what?" She did not bother to look at the goblin as he scrambled after her.

"I am sorry."

Annie ignored the goblin. She found her way back to the clearing on the edge of the mire where she had found the tracks and the torn dish towel and began scrutinizing the surrounding brush for any sign of a new trail.

"Only wanted my wee changelin'," Kull said, sitting down on a fallen tree trunk. "Didn'a mean any harm ta yer manling. Honest."

"Your changeling?" Annie rounded on him. "Yours? They are *my* boys."

"The changelin' isn'a—"

"Have you sung any lullabies in the past thirteen years?" she demanded. "Helped anyone with their homework? Taught anyone how to tie their father's old bow ties with fumbling fingers so they could dress up for their first school dance?"

Kull opened his mouth, and then tactfully closed it.

"Mm-hm. My boys."

They searched wordlessly through the bushes for the next few minutes. It was Kull who broke the silence. "They went this way," he said.

Annie glared at the goblin before climbing out along the long tree trunk where he stood. Muddy footprints marked the children's path.

"Ya read my message?" Kull asked softly from behind her.

"I read it."

"Then ya already know."

Annie stared at the footprints.

"Iffin the changelin' doesn'a come back ta the horde this night, then it doesn'a matter whose boy he is."

"I'm going to find them," said Annie.

SIXTEEN

"YOU SHOULDN'T GO THAT WAY," FABLE'S VOICE
called down at the boys from high above them.

"We're not listening to you anymore!" Tinn snapped,
continuing his angry trek toward the heart of the forest.

Fable hopped from branch to branch, tree to tree. She
was keeping up easily, free from the viny undergrowth.
"You're going to get lost."

"Lost? Imagine that." Tinn glowered and kept moving
forward. He was maddest at himself for opening up to a
total stranger about everything.

"If you want—"

"We don't need you. We don't *want* you—go away!"

"But—" Fable stopped abruptly, as if struck. "But we're friends now."

Tinn let out an exasperated grunt and threw his hands up, stomping off without a response.

"You should go home, Fable," Cole called up at her, a little more gently. "We're going to the other side of the Oddmire. It wouldn't be safe for you anyway. We'll find our own way from here."

Fable pursed her lips and scowled as Cole hurried to catch up with his brother. For a long while, the boys did not hear another word out of her. From time to time, out of the corner of his eye, Cole caught a flicker of curly hair slipping along the branches above them. He found the sight strangely comforting, in spite of Tinn's continued grumbling.

Gradually, the trees began to thin and the air began to thicken. Heavy fog rolled along the spongy earth, and the boys knew they had found the Oddmire once again.

Tinn came to a stop right at the edge of the murky swamp, and Cole drew up beside him.

"I don't see any sort of bridge," said Tinn.

"I can't even see the other side, can you?" Cole said.

Tinn shook his head. He found a knobby tree branch almost as tall as he was and lowered it into the inscrutable green water. It did not touch the bottom. When he tried to pull it out again, the mire sucked at it until eventually he gave up the fight and just let the mire have it.

Here and there, tree trunks jutted out of the swamp, their bark coated in moss and slime. It was anyone's guess how far their roots sank below the surface before they found solid earth. Five feet? Fifty? The trees grew fainter and fainter the farther out they stood, fading into the distance until they were enveloped completely by the thick gray haze. Cole guessed the farthest he could see was a hundred feet out, maybe less. Even if the shore was just beyond his clouded vision—it would still be like swimming through pancake batter to get there. His head spun just breathing in the heady mist rolling off the Oddmire.

"Maybe we could make a raft out of logs?" Cole said, although he wasn't sure how well a raft would work on water that was mostly made out of mud—besides which, all of the logs within eyesight looked as if they were half-mud themselves.

"There's something out there," said Tinn. He pointed out into the murk.

Cole tried to follow his gaze. The rolling fog made strange shapes dance at the limits of his vision; gray ships on gray waves melted into coiled gray dragons, which folded into skeletal gray faces. "It's just the mist," Cole murmured.

"It isn't. There. See it? What is that?"

Cole blinked hard and looked again. A tiny pinprick of flickering orange light cut through the mist. "Is that a lantern?" His heartbeat quickened. "Maybe there's a house on the other side?"

"No, it's moving. Watch."

The tiny light jiggled and jumped, inching forward. Briefly, Cole imagined he had seen a hint of a shadow beside it. An arm? A pair of legs beneath?

"Someone's crossing!" Cole said. If someone was crossing, that meant there was a way to cross. He and Tinn exchanged glances full of excitement and fear. Sure enough, the little flickering light was growing brighter as it traversed the swamp. It was not bound straight for them, but toward the shore some ways up the bank, and the boys hurried across the soggy ground to reach the spot.

"Ugh. Nothing over this way," Annie Burton grunted. For the dozenth time, the children's trail had tapered off, and she and Kull had been forced to scan the surrounding forest for any sign of them.

"Na this way, either," Kull called, tromping back toward her, slapping leaves out of his face. "Otch! Mind yer feet, womern," Kull warned.

Annie glanced down just in time to avoid catching her ankle on a creeping, thorny vine.

The goblin hissed through his jagged teeth. "'Tis a bit o' the wicked bramble, that is," he said. "They're much worse in the Deep Dark, but them vines run all through the Wild Wood. Nasty things."

"Oh, stop it. They're just vines. Keep looking. I'm going back this way—I saw a building up ahead. It looks like an old run-down cabin. If the boys came this way, maybe they found it, too."

"Wait!" Kull drew to a full stop, his hands out and his eyes wide.

"What now? Was I about to step on a pointy pebble?"

"This is a witchin' place," whispered the goblin.

"What? Seriously?" Annie glanced around. Kull's tone was unsettling, but the real world was the real world and stories were stories. "You mean the Witch of the Wood? Queen of the Deep Dark? That's real?"

Kull pointed to an ancient piece of sun-bleached, knotted rope halfway up the nearest tree. "Witchies' knots." He chewed on his bottom lip. "We shouldn'a be here," he said.

Annie let her eyes slide down the trunk. There, near the bottom of the tree, a fresh notch had been cut in the shape of a jagged C. "The boys have been here," she said. "Come on."

Cole and Tinn were crouched behind a fallen tree when the figure from the fog finally reached the shore of the Oddmire. He could not have been more than three feet tall—a man, or male, at least, and very old. This much they surmised from the enormous peppery beard that burst thickly from his face and did not stop until it was dragging on the ground near his toes. The beard was so full and bushy that the man's short, thin body was almost entirely hidden behind it, like an afterthought to the facial hair. Two scrawny arms stuck out from the sides of the beard and two dirty bare feet padded along the earth beneath it, but the figure's torso was completely lost to the hairy nest. From out of the top of the bushy mess peeked a wide nose, two squinting eyes, and a very bald head.

In the center of the strange man's beard, like a robin's nest tucked in the knothole of a tree, was the source of the light: a single stout candle shone from within the wiry hair. The beard glowed around the flame, light flickering through its curls, but it did not appear to burn. Ivory trails of wax trickled below the candle and made themselves a part of the mighty beard.

The man faltered as he moved, taking small, hesitant steps toward the forest and casting glances back at the swamp. He had not yet spotted the boys. A bright yellow butterfly flitted through trees beside him, and the man froze. His eyes went wide and his nostrils flared. His mustache hairs wiggled as he panted, watching the little insect flutter across the clearing.

Tinn and Cole looked at each other, then back at the strange old man.

The butterfly was three feet away from him when he suddenly exploded into motion, grasping for the little thing like a cat swiping at a fly. He almost had it once or twice, but the butterfly climbed above his reach and up into the forest canopy.

The old man cursed under his breath. He leaned his hands on his knees, looking defeated.

Cole screwed up his courage and stood up. "Um. Hi," he said.

The little man jumped, made a startled noise that sounded a bit like a donkey sneezing, tried to throw himself backward and sideways at the same time, tripped over his own feet, and finally spun headlong into a mossy stump. He sat there, dazed for a moment, looking like an unruly pile of damp hair.

"It's okay!" Cole said, holding out his hands in what he hoped was a reassuring gesture. Tinn stepped out to join him.

"Hey, mister. We're not going to hurt you. We're friendly."

"We just want to talk to you," added Cole. "About the swamp."

The man wobbled and gazed up at the twins. He blinked rapidly and then looked from one to the other and back again. He squinted, shook his head, and raised one bushy eyebrow. Slowly, he held up two fingers.

"Two?" said Tinn. "Yeah, there's two of us. We're twins."

Satisfied, the man nodded and let the hand drop.

"I'm Cole," said Cole. "And this is Tinn. What's your name?"

The man's eyes darted between them. The flame at his chest danced wildly, although neither of the boys could feel a breeze. He did not respond.

"They don't use names," said a voice above them, and Fable dropped down to the ground right behind the boys with a soft thump. The skittish figure at their feet gave a startled yelp and pressed backward against the stump.

"And they hardly ever talk, either," added Fable. "Except to each other. They're called hinkypunks. Used to be lots of them in the forest. Lots of other magical forest folk, too. They pretty much all left, though. Even the gnomes left."

The little man pushed himself up to his full if unimposing height and straightened his beard, looking through

104

narrowed eyes at the three children. With a slightly accusatory expression on his face, he held up three fingers.

"Oh. Yeah, there are actually three of us, I guess," said Tinn. Behind him, Fable did not try to hide her smile. "That one's called Fable. She's annoying, but she's not gonna hurt you, either. So what do we call you?"

The man pursed his lips, furrowing his brow as he scratched behind his ear.

"Hinkypunks just are what they are," Fable said. "They haven't got names."

"They must've called each other something," said Cole, "back when there was more than one of them."

"Come to think of it, where did they go?" said Fable, leaning in toward the old man. "All the other hinkypunks and the spriggans and pixies and stuff—do you know where they went? Mama said you all had to leave, but she didn't say why. And how come you didn't go with them?"

The hinkypunk's candle dimmed and flickered. He glanced at Fable, and his shoulders sagged.

"You didn't want them to go without you, did you?" said Tinn. "And now you're all alone?"

The odd man just stared at the ground and heaved a sigh. His brow cast a heavy shadow over his eyes.

"Look. Um. We need to get to the other side of the Oddmire," Cole said.

The man's gaze flicked to the swamp.

"We saw you crossing. Do you think you could show us the way?"

The hinkypunk's eyes widened for a moment, and he looked as if he would like to climb right out of his own hair and run away.

"I like your beard," said Fable. "And your candle. I'm gonna call you Candlebeard, okay?"

The hinkypunk raised his head a fraction. He shrugged.

"Will you take us to the other side?" Fable asked.

Candlebeard glanced at the swamp. He swallowed.

"I'm really sorry about your family," said Tinn softly. "I wish we could help you."

Candlebeard nodded glumly.

"But if you helped us, it might just help all the magical creatures left in the Wild Wood. It would definitely help my family. You see, it's really important that we get to the other side of the Oddmire. It would mean an awful lot if you would show us the way."

Candlebeard pursed his lips. Very gradually, he raised his hand. It trembled just a little. He was holding up four fingers.

"Yeah," said Tinn. "The four of us."

SEVENTEEN

CANDLEBEARD STEPPED OUT INTO THE MURKY
mire and planted one muddy foot firmly on nothing at all.
At least, to the boys it appeared to be nothing at all. His
toes sank just beneath the surface of the swamp and then
held steady.

He glanced back and gestured for the children to follow. His candle flame bobbed hazily in the reflection
beneath him, and then he turned again and hopped a few
feet farther along. Where his foot had been, the murky
water bubbled and the faintest dimple remained, like a
fingerprint left in rising bread dough.

Cole looked at Tinn. "Well. Here goes," he said.

"Wait," said Tinn, but Cole was already stepping out into the swirling water of the mire. He planted his foot on the fading patch that was the hinkypunk's footprint. His boot sank an inch or so under the foamy gray-green surface, but then he found himself standing firmly a few feet out from the shore.

"There's a step!" he exclaimed. "A stump or a stone or something—it's just beneath the water!"

Candlebeard had already moved two or three steps farther along the hidden route.

"Hey! Wait up!" Cole called.

Candlebeard could not hear him, or else did not listen. He hopped forward again. Back on the shore, Tinn bit his lip, shifting from one foot to the other as Cole jumped after the hinkypunk.

"It's okay." Fable smiled gamely. "Go ahead. I'll be right behind you guys."

"Whether we want you to or not, huh?" Tinn took a deep breath.

Fable laughed. "Yup." She squeezed her eyes shut and then popped them open.

"What are you doing?"

"I'm winking. It's a people thing that makes friends feel better and like you more."

"That's not winking. That's—I don't know what that is. Don't do that."

"Is it working, though?"

"Come on, Tinn!" Cole urged from up ahead. He took another step, and his foot half missed the invisible landing. He flung out his arm, swaying as he struggled to keep his balance.

Tinn held his breath and took the first step after them. And then another. Cole was three or four paces ahead, Candlebeard nearly a dozen. Tinn's heart was thudding, but with each step that did not drown him in the bubbling mud, his confidence grew.

There was a rhythm to it. Ahead of him, Cole bobbed forward, to the left, and forward again. In turn, Tinn hopped forward, left, forward. It was beginning to feel like a dance.

For a fraction of a second, Tinn's mind flickered to the only actual dance he had ever experienced. He had stood with Cole on the back wall of the grange hall until Hana Sakai had come over in her fancy dress and asked if one of them would like to dance—to which Tinn had naturally choked on his own spit and erupted in a fit of coughs. Cole had danced with Hana while Tinn had sputtered, for which Tinn had felt quite grateful. Then, after a while, he had begun to feel something else. It wasn't jealousy—he never felt jealous of his brother. His brother's triumphs and failures had always felt like his own—but it was something new. He had scanned the far side of the hall until he had found Evie Warner. The feeling, whatever it was, had gotten stronger.

Tinn had fumbled his way across the dance floor until he was standing directly in front of Evie. She had looked up at him with a baffled expression that mirrored the strange, uncertain feelings inside him, and then, plucking up his courage, he had . . . not asked her to dance. He had not managed to say anything at all. The two of them had just stared at each other awkwardly until the song ended and the crowd around them applauded the band.

Tinn tried to remember if he had even reached out for Evie's hand before the whole thing was suddenly over. The thought had certainly crossed his mind. Tinn was not good at dancing.

Ahead of him in the misty Oddmire, Cole had gotten half a dozen jumps ahead.

Yes, this awful swamp was painfully like a dance, Tinn decided. He wondered briefly what Evie Warner might be doing right now—and as he was wondering, he missed his next step. His leg plunged straight into the mire, and the acrid mud leapt up to catch him full in the face. Tinn's world was suddenly dark and wet and heavy, his lungs were burning, and there was no air.

It has been said that sharks can smell a single drop of blood from a mile away. Like many interesting and unbelievable facts, this one is not true—but knowing that it is not true will be of little comfort to the shipwrecked, bleeding swimmer who has just spotted fins on the watery horizon. More true, and also more terrifying, is the fact that there are things far worse than being sniffed out by a hungry shark—including truly gruesome creatures who make the toothiest sharks look like cuddly kittens.

What Tinn did not know, as his body sank deeper into the mire, was that such a creature had already caught his scent—not his blood, but his fear. The smell of his utter panic and his exquisite distress rippled through the Oddmire until it reached the Thing.

Perhaps it was best that Tinn did not know that his fear was drawing the Thing nearer with every flailing wave of his hands. Such knowledge could only have caused him greater distress—and at the moment, Tinn was quite distressed enough simply attempting to breathe.

The Thing grinned wickedly. The Thing waited for the children to draw just a little closer.

EIGHTEEN

"THROUGH HERE," ANNIE SAID. "THE LEAVES ARE all broken and stomped down. Do you think they were trying to leave us a trail?"

"I dinna think them daft boys know what they're doin' at all. Beginnin' ta think they're tryin' to cover every last inch o' the Wild Wood *except* the safe, simple path I left 'em."

"We're getting close to the mire again. God, that muck stinks."

"I drew them fools a map! Do humans na know how maps work? Spent days gettin' it just right!"

"Did you hear something?" Annie drew to a stop. Ahead of them, the trees thinned, fog rolling in off the swampy waters of the mire.

"Learnt a whole new alphabet, I did! An' fancy words ta go with it. But can they be bothered ta follow a simple path?"

"Stop talking!" Annie squinted out into the fog.

"Oh, they'd na be out there," Kull said. "'Tis the Oddmire, that is. Lose yer way just tryin' ta stand still out in that mist, and na bridges around fer half a mile or more."

"BOYS!" Annie began vaulting over the bushes as she ran. "Tinn! Cole!"

"Ya daffy womern, what—" And then Kull saw them, too. "Otch! Boys!" he yelled. They were fifty yards away, taking little hops farther and farther into the mist. The twins were trailed by a girl with curly hair Kull did not recognize. Ahead of them, a pinprick of light bobbed forward over the waters of the mire. When Kull realized what he was seeing, he cursed in Goblish.

"Cole!" Annie cried again. "Tinn!" The fog choked her screams, and they bounced back to her over the murky water in muffled, unintelligible echoes.

Mere feet from the water's edge, Kull caught up with her, latching onto the woman's arm and pulling her back before she could plunge into the mire.

"Let go of me! What are you doing?"

The figures were vanishing into the distance, the clouds of fog rolling in hungrily to engulf them.

113

"Ya canna help me get my changelin' back if yer dead, womern!"

"But the boys—"

"Them fool boys are followin' a hinky! Otch! Dinna humans have any sense at all? Why would anyone ever follow a hinky? Of course, that bearded blighter will know how ta get across, but 'tis anyone's guess if them idjits will still be with him when he does."

The mist spun, forming eldritch shapes in the distance, and Annie's head began to swim. She felt sick. The whole world was beginning to tip, and she couldn't tell if it was the fog or her frustration that was causing it.

"What do I do?" she moaned. "You know so much about this stupid forest—what do I do?"

"We go back ta the beginning," said Kull. "We take the goblin bridge. Better the long way than the dead way. If we're right quick, maybe we can meet 'em on t'other side before they've gotten far."

"And if that hinky-thing decides to drown my boys in the mire before they ever reach the other side?"

Kull's pained grimace and a heavy sigh were his only response.

With one last glance at the rolling fog that had swallowed her children, Annie nodded to Kull, and up the bank they ran.

NINETEEN

Tɪɴɴ ɢᴀsᴘᴇᴅ. ᴛʜᴇ ᴍᴜᴄᴋ ᴡᴀs sᴛɪʟʟ ᴛʜɪᴄᴋ ᴏᴠᴇʀ his eyes, but he could feel solid ground beneath him now and fresh air on his skin. He was out of the mire. He remembered splashing, struggling, sinking, but not surfacing. Had he passed out? His breath came now in hungry, frantic gulps, as though he was afraid the mist around him would steal the air away again at any moment. To be fair, in the thick of the Oddmire, that was a distinct possibility.

"He's breathing!" Fable's voice yelled from somewhere close by. "You're breathing, Tinn! Keep doing that!"

Cole breathed, too. He wasn't even sure how long he had been holding his breath. Had he breathed when Fable was vaulting the hidden steps to reach Tinn before he sank? Had he breathed when Candlebeard materialized beside her, the tip of his beard trailing in the grimy water as he hauled Tinn up by his ankles? Had he breathed while he was watching the two strange forest people rescue his brother?

Cole had frozen when his brother needed him most. The best he had been able to do was to lean out of their way as Candlebeard and Fable hoisted Tinn out of the muck and carried him along the secret steps to a flat, soggy island in the middle of the mire. The island was no wider than a kitchen table, but it had room for the sputtering child to lie flat with just enough space left for his three companions to hover.

Tinn sat up, coughing wetly and wiping mud out of his eyes. Cole took the moment to finally look around at the site where Candlebeard had led them. He couldn't tell if the mist had gotten denser here, or if his eyes were watering. Possibly both. There was no sign of the shore in any direction. He tried to fix his gaze on a tree about ten yards away, but the trunk seemed to bend and twist under the weight of his attention. Anywhere he looked, the swampy surroundings curled and swayed, refusing to stay in focus.

For just a moment, Cole was sure he heard voices crying out through the fog. He could have sworn he heard his mother, calling for him as she had a million times from the back window. Then on top of his mother's voice drifted another, rough and raspy, and then a third, ladylike and courtly and cold. Voices began to bounce around him on all sides, echoing and overlapping—muffled words and shouts and eerie laughter, and behind them all rose a deep, low growl.

"You hear them, too?" whispered Fable, sliding up to his shoulder. "Mama says the Oddmire talks to people. It tries to turn them about." Fable looked around nervously. "What are they saying to you?"

Cole shook his head. He tried to concentrate on the sound of his mother's voice, but now all the voices were weaving in and out like complicated knots, gradually fading to hums and hisses. The mist curled and swirled, a wall of suffocating gray.

"I don't know," said Cole. The voice that could have been his mother's was melting into nothing, overtaken again by the low buzz and burble of the swamp itself. "Nothing, I guess. I just . . ." He let the thought trail off.

"I heard her, too," said Tinn. Cole turned to face his brother, who had pushed himself up to standing. Tinn was coated from head to toe in green sludge, but he was steady enough on his feet.

"Heard who?" breathed Fable.

"Mom," said Cole.

"The queen," said Tinn at the same moment.

The twins stared at each other.

"The queen?" said Cole. "You think?"

Tinn nodded, soberly. "And I think she's angry."

"What queen?" Fable asked, her voice still a murmur.

"*The* queen," Tinn said. "The Queen of the Deep Dark, Witch of the Wild Wood, Mother of Monsters. You really never heard the stories growing up?"

Fable shrugged and shook her head.

"How do you know it was her?" said Cole.

Tinn pursed his lips. "Just a feeling, I guess."

"How do you even know there is a witch in the Wild Wood?" said Fable, crinkling her nose. "You guys keep talking about her, but I've lived here my whole life and I've never met some evil queen who eats people and bites crops."

"Blights crops."

"She sounds made up. I don't think she exists."

The queen did exist. She was more real, more powerful, and more dangerous than the twins had ever dared to daydream. Of their motley party, in fact, only one of them truly fathomed the sheer force of nature that was the Witch of the Wild Wood, and that was Candlebeard.

Candlebeard had heard her, too. He did not offer the children his opinion about the witch, however. He did not

118

tell the children, for instance, that his people had their own stories about the witch. He did not tell them that their title for the witch was neither *Queen* nor *Mother* of anything, but something much stronger that had no translation in any human tongue. Candlebeard did not tell the children that the witch chilled him to his very core. Most of all, he did not tell them that his fear of the witch was the reason he was now running away without them, abandoning the children, helpless and unescorted, in the middle of the misty, murky Oddmire.

"Hey!" yelled Cole. The others turned in time to see the trembling hinkypunk racing off into the mist. "Wait! Come back!"

Cole and Tinn and Fable managed to follow for half a dozen sodden steps before Candlebeard's path became indiscernible. The glow of his candle bobbed farther and farther away until it faded off into the haze completely, and the surface of the mire refused to surrender any more signs of his passing.

"Wait!" Cole wailed once more. "Come back!"

Candlebeard had vanished. Cole put one foot forward and dipped it into the swamp. His searching boot found nothing solid beneath the surface. He tried again to the left and right, but the swamp held fast to its secrets.

Cole looked as if he wanted to cry.

"This is farther than I've ever gotten before," said Fable quietly.

"It's as far as any of us is going to get," said Tinn.

There the children stayed, rooted to their submerged steps for several long moments. Or minutes. Or possibly hours. It was impossible to tell in the mists of the Oddmire.

A very clever, scientifically minded man with a lot of shiny telescoping instruments and a tweed coat with elbow patches had once tried to document the phenomenon of the Oddmire, long before the boys were born. His goal had been to determine if the Madness of the Mire actually warped the passage of time or simply the perceptions of the traveler. His results were inconclusive, however, owing to the fact that he was not found until three weeks later, wandering through the cornfields of a town fifty miles to the south, quite naked and mumbling about squirrels. His shiny instruments were found two months after that on the roof of a cowshed, missing several important parts.

The children remained rooted to the swampy steps until their legs ached. At last, Cole took a deep breath. He was preparing to swim across the mire toward the nearest shore. At least, he was preparing to swim across the mire toward what he *guessed* might be the nearest shore. In truth, he had no idea in which direction the nearest shore might lie, but doing nothing was not something Cole had ever been very good at.

Before he could plunge in, a sound echoed across the fetid muck. It was a creaking, groaning sound, accompanied by the splash of something moving through the water. A low wave, scarcely more than a ripple, washed over their feet. Tinn straightened. "What was that?" he said.

The mist ahead of them parted as though cut by an enormous knife, each side peeling away to form a valley of visibility.

"Oh," said Fable. "Oh, dang."

"What?" said Cole. "What's happening?"

"Trouble," Fable whispered.

The twins stared at the corridor of clarity in bewilderment as drab, grimy roots bubbled to the surface of the Oddmire. The slimy stalks knit themselves together, forming a narrow path all the way to the shore—which, Cole and Tinn could finally see, lay not thirty feet away.

The glistening gray roots drew to a stop directly in front of Fable. "Big, big trouble." She winced, sighed, and put a foot gingerly out onto the braided platform. It held her weight. Step by grudging step, she crossed the swamp for the shore. "Come on, guys."

Cole was the first to follow, hoping nobody noticed that the shoreline was exactly opposite the direction he had been preparing to swim. The passageway beneath his feet was slick and uneven, and it bobbed up and down with each step, as if the whole swamp was breathing. The motion made Cole's stomach turn, but the bridge held firm. Tinn brought up the rear. Glancing back, he saw the roots behind him sinking into the mire from whence they came, and he quickened his pace.

When they were nearly to the shore, Cole spotted a figure at last. At first he mistook it for a man, big and burly and covered in woolly, matted furs. As he stepped closer, leaving behind the heady fog of the mire at last, his eyes found focus and he stopped dead.

Tinn drew up beside him. "No way."

The bear was exactly as enormous as the boys remembered it. Its teeth were long and its eyes piercing. It stood on its hind feet, towering over them, as steam rose in thick clouds from its flanks into the chilly air—an effect that only served to make the monster even more unnaturally frightening. The bear sneered.

"Seriously?" Tinn said. "Are you *still* following us? We didn't even do anything to your cub!"

Fable began to cross the grass toward the beast.

"Whoa! What are you doing?" said Cole, but the girl continued forward. The bear dropped down as she approached. And then the animal did something neither boy would ever be able to properly describe. There was something of a rearing-up motion—or maybe it was a sort of swooping motion—definitely a tossing-back motion, and the figure standing before them was suddenly not a bear at all.

A hood of thick, dark fur rested on the woman's shoulders. The bearskin cloak continued to billow hot steam. The woman's eyes remained piercing. Cole could not stop himself from wondering if her teeth were just as sharp as the bear's.

"You—you're her. You're the Witch of the Wood, aren't you?" Tinn managed.

Fable glanced at him, startled, and then back to the woman.

"If you like," said the witch.

"The Queen of the Deep Dark," croaked Cole.

"I've always rather liked that one." The witch smiled.

"Wait, *you're* the 'Mother of Monsters' they've been talking about?" Fable asked the woman.

"I suppose—but isn't every mother? Have you met children?"

"And you're also . . . a bear?" said Tinn.

"I am as my forest needs me to be."

"Are you a person that turns into a bear," Cole asked, "or a bear that turns into a person?"

The queen narrowed her eyes at him. "That depends," she said, "on how you define a person."

"Can you be other things?" asked Tinn. "You're bigger as a bear. Could you be smaller? Like a ladybug or something?"

"So that two crafty young boys could catch me and put me in a bottle, I suppose?" said the queen, one eyebrow arching up. "And not let me out unless I promise to grant them wishes and let them go free?"

"What? No," said Tinn. "I wasn't thinking anything like that."

"A shame." She shrugged. "It would have been quite clever of you."

"We haven't got any bottles, anyhow," said Cole. "I had a dish towel, but I dropped it when—well, when we met you, I guess. Oh, and we really didn't do anything to that cub, by the way, I promise!"

"Except rescue it," added Tinn, "from the mire."

The witch smirked. "You three have been having quite the adventure all across my forest, haven't you?" she said icily. "But, like all adventures must, yours has now come to an end."

"No," said Fable.

The witch turned very slowly to face her. Her brow rose a fraction as she fixed the trembling girl with an iron gaze. "No?"

"We're on a quest," Fable squeaked. "It's important."

"It is," said Cole. "We need to cross the Deep Dark together."

The witch's eyes flashed to him.

"Please," said Tinn.

For just a moment, the queen's resolve seemed to soften ever so slightly.

Fable seized the moment. "They *need* to," she pressed. "And I'm helping them. See, it's like this: one of these boys isn't a boy at all, he's a changeling, and he needs to find the goblins before—"

"What naughty little children *need* to do," the queen said, cutting her off sharply, her moment of softness whipping away like a snuffed candle, "is to stop talking back!" She waved her hand, and Tinn and Cole felt the air around them grow heavier and heavier, pressing down like a thick, leaden blanket. Tinn's vision dimmed. His knees gave out and he collapsed to the forest floor. Cole took half a step toward him before the trees swam around him and the forest darkened.

The last thing the boys could hear before they lost consciousness completely was the sound of measured footsteps and Fable's timid voice.

"I'm sorry," she whimpered.

"Big," replied the witch, "*big* trouble."

TWENTY

KULL CRESTED THE HILL AND IMMEDIATELY dropped to his belly against the prickly grass. Annie lowered her head and caught up with him in a crouch.

"What is it?" she whispered.

"Otch, stay down," he hissed. "That's the queenie up ahead."

"Queenie? What are you talking—" And then Annie saw. She stood up.

"Ya daft womern. I said down!" rasped Kull.

Annie did not get down. In the clearing ahead, a strange woman stood over her boys. The woman wore a cloak of thick, dark furs. Beside her cowered a child Annie did not recognize, a girl, agitated and disheveled, with wild curly hair. She couldn't make out their words, but her twins were speaking to the woman.

"Those are my boys," Annie breathed.

Now the queen was saying something to the children, but Annie still could not hear any voices from atop the craggy hill. Abruptly, the woman waved her hand, the air rippled, and Tinn and Cole crumpled to the sodden ground.

"Those are my boys," Annie repeated numbly. She started forward.

Kull pulled at the hem of her skirt, shaking his head, his eyes nervous and pleading. Annie hardly noticed him.

Down in the clearing, the queen had turned her attention to the remaining child. The girl looked about the same age as Annie's boys. The horrible woman spoke again and pointed a finger squarely at the girl's chest. The girl spun away, but before her back was to the queen she had already begun to change. She trembled and doubled over, and then the girl was not a girl at all. She had become an animal, covered in rich, dark fur just like the woman's cloak.

Annie blanched. Was that poor, frightened child fated to become the wicked woman's next garment? A matching shawl, perhaps? The queen turned her attention back to the motionless twins.

Annie Burton's fists clenched, her teeth ground, her legs pumped, and the craggy hillside swept beneath her.

"Those," she growled loudly, "are *my* boys!"

The queen looked up. She blinked. The Queen of the Deep Dark, Witch of the Wild Wood, Mother of Monsters—was not expecting Annie Burton.

Candlebeard crouched low behind a prickly bush. He chewed on the ends of his mustache as his stomach twisted and tightened. He should not have come back. He should have left long ago—should have run far away with the rest of the hinkypunks and never come back to this terrible forest at all. But it was too late for that.

At the queen's will, the boys had collapsed to the ground not twenty feet from where Candlebeard was hiding. He cringed. The witch looked away, raising her hand to point at the little forest girl. "Big, *big* trouble," she said. There was a whimper and a muffled pop and then Candlebeard could not see the girl anymore. He could smell the witchy magic in the air—earthen and very human, but sharp with the power of the otherworld, too.

The boys lay lifeless between Candlebeard and the witch. No, not lifeless. He could see their chests rise and fall with shallow breaths. A nervous idea began to pace back and forth in Candlebeard's mind. He shook his head to dislodge it, but the idea continued to march unbidden through his thoughts.

The witch turned back to the boys, and Candlebeard saw her face clearly for the first time. He held his breath. He had never been so close to the witch before—and he could only hope that she did not see him. He held his hands in front of his candle, willing his own flame to dim. The witch looked about thirty years old, or possibly sixty-five? Not a day over ninety—Candlebeard had never been particularly good at judging ages, especially those of short-lived humans who couldn't be bothered to grow proper beards. The woman was pretty enough, he supposed, as humans go. She had hard features and dark, smoky hair, but her expression was cold and forbidding.

Her icy gaze rose a fraction to pierce the gloom of the forest, and Candlebeard's heart dropped. Had she heard him? Could she hear his heart pounding even now? See his flame flickering?

And then, abruptly, she turned away again. Candlebeard breathed. On the opposite side of the clearing, a human woman was running down the hill toward them. She ran clumsily, not minding her step, her eyes fixed on the queen.

The queen cocked her head at the woman's approach. Intrigued, the queen stepped toward her—away from the boys, and away from Candlebeard.

Every inch of Candlebeard's body shuddered. He could have been with his people right now, he thought miserably. He could have been far away from this terrible forest, never looking back. He had missed his chance back then. He would not miss it now. The nervous idea that had been pacing back and forth in his mind saw its opportunity and clambered hastily down into his feet. Candlebeard took a deep breath and crept out from behind the prickly bush.

Kull could only watch, mortified. Annie Burton did not fall down the hill, exactly. She stumbled, yes, tripping on several rocks and viny plants, but she did not fall. Gravity was no match for Annie Burton's fury, and she would not give it the satisfaction of halting her approach.

Above her, Kull clawed at his own cheeks in indecision. There was no reason to join her in her madness. What was she thinking? And what was to be gained? It wasn't as though the woman had more on the line than Kull. The whole of the goblin horde would wither and die if that changeling never made it through the forest. This was about so much more than two stupid children.

Kull let his hands drop to his sides.

But it *was* about two stupid children, as well. They were the two stupid children Kull had watched over for almost thirteen years. They were the stupid children he had protected, weaving goblin charms to keep their rickety tree fort from collapsing, to keep the wolves that wandered the edge of the woods from prowling too close, to keep the dam upstream from cracking—it was a human-built dam, shoddy even by their standards, and should have burst and flooded the town a decade ago. Kull had made the repairs himself. He had watched out for those stupid children. They were his stupid children. At least, one of them was his.

Kull steeled himself. He drew himself up to his full four feet and seven inches and climbed over the ledge after Annie Burton.

The queen took slow, measured steps to meet the intruders at the foot of the hill. She suppressed a smile.

Directly in front of her, the furious human, Annie Burton, planted her feet on solid ground at last, her teeth clenched and her fists balled. The little goblin halted and steeled himself several feet behind, looking as resolute as he could, the precious thing.

"Those are my boys," Annie growled.

"I heard you the first time," the queen replied lazily. "And you are wrong."

Annie breathed through her teeth. She looked as if she might throw herself at the witch at any moment.

"One of the boys is yours," the queen continued. "Just one. Isn't that right? The other—" She eyed Kull. "Well, I assume you had something to do with that, didn't you, little thief?"

Kull blanched.

"A changeling. It has been a long time. But you came back for it, didn't you—came back for your lost wayward monster?" She pursed her lips, considering. "How unlike a goblin. If I thought it possible for one of your kind to care about a child's life, I might be deceived into believing that he meant something to you."

"Means everythin'," Kull croaked.

"I find that very hard to believe, thief. Unless—I suppose you have something to gain from the poor creature's return?"

Kull did not answer.

"Quite a lot to gain?"

Kull's eyes fell.

"That does explain it. Small wonder that they were fleeing into my forest rather than back to the likes of you. You know, I think they might prefer life in the Wild Wood, don't you?"

"No. I won't let you turn my boys into animals," Annie Burton said. "You can't have them."

The queen let a smile spread freely across her face now, equal parts amused and impressed. "So bold," she said. "My dear, sweet, stupid woman, you really believe you have a say in this, don't you?"

Annie only glared. They locked eyes, and the witch's smile melted slowly into something softer, a strange spark of tenderness glittering behind her gaze as she appraised the woman.

"If you really care so very much," she said, stiffening, "can you even identify your own child?"

Annie scowled and glanced at Kull. Kull bit his lip. In thirteen long years, for all his studying and spying, Kull had never been certain which child was his marvelous changeling and which was the unmagical human.

"You can't, can you? You both wish to claim your poor, lost children, but you don't even know them, do you? Well, I do." The queen lowered her chin. Hard shadows fell under her brow. "I know lost children. And I will make you a deal. If either one of you can guess correctly—if either one of you can claim your true kin, then I will give you back your child. Simple as that. You will be free to leave my forest with him and never look back."

Kull brightened. Annie remained less than satisfied.

"But whichever you choose," the queen finished, "the other will be forfeited to me."

Candlebeard kept himself low, thanking the uneven ground and the bushes for what scarce cover they provided him as he moved. The witch's back was still turned. She was talking to the two intruders.

Candlebeard plucked a pebble from the ground and tossed it at the nearest slumbering boy. It bounced off Tinn's cheek and his nose twitched. Candlebeard glanced back up at the adults.

"That's not acceptable," Annie Burton was saying.

"Don't tell *me* it's not," said the queen, calmly, although Candlebeard could hear the tightness in her voice. "Tell your cowering compatriot, there. That's the standard bargain, isn't it? One child taken, the other left behind? That's how it works. What do you say, thief—do you know your own blood well enough to choose?"

Kull took a hesitant step forward, then faltered, gnawing on his lip. "Iffin I choose wrong?"

"Then your precious changeling belongs to the forest."

Kull opened his mouth and then closed it again, his expression visibly pained. "That's na very fair."

"No," agreed the queen pointedly, "it's not."

Behind the witch, Candlebeard held his breath as he reached a trembling hand out toward the nearest boy.

Hinkypunks, like all manner of fairies and oddlings, have *glamour*, the magical camouflage with which they hide themselves from mortal eyes. Candlebeard concentrated harder than he could ever remember on maintaining his glamour now. He was confident that he was invisible to the human, and probably to the goblin, as well—but it was neither the human nor the goblin he feared. He did not fully understand the Queen of the Deep Dark, and he did not wish to remain in her company long enough to learn more. He shook Cole's shoulder. The boy only murmured softly in his sleep.

The queen turned her head to look.

Candlebeard felt the blood in his veins turn to ice. He was completely exposed, and she was looking right at him, her expression unchanging. Could she see him?

And then the human, Annie, spoke again. "I know."

The queen turned back around. Candlebeard breathed. It took everything he had in him not to collapse then and there.

"You know?" the queen said.

"I've always known," said Annie.

The Queen of the Deep Dark turned her eyes to Annie Burton.

"You're ready to make a guess, then?"

"No," said Annie. "Not a guess. A fact. A mother knows her children, and I know my boys. Both of them."

The queen raised an eyebrow. "*Both* is not a choice."

"Of course it's not! Why on earth would I choose? I don't care which one has my blood and which one doesn't. I don't care which one I pushed into this world with his father at my side, and which one was born far away to some goblin mother and father—"

"Actually, there's an egg," Kull began. "Father's na decided until—"

"I don't care! Those are both my boys, and if you tell me that even one of them will be staying in this horrible forest, then you had better get very used to me, because I'm staying, too." Annie took another step closer to the witch, refusing to be cowed. "I am not," she said, planting her fists on her hips, "leaving these woods without them."

The queen did not back up. She did not scowl or sneer or snarl. She smiled. "Good answer."

Annie Burton blinked.

Kull lifted his head.

"Take your children," said the witch. Her face turned toward the sunlight for a moment, and she looked almost pleasant. "Both of them."

Annie Burton's lips fell open.

"Huh," said Kull. A jagged smile cut across his face. "That was a test, wasn' it?"

"And the girl," said Annie Burton.

The witch raised an eyebrow. "The girl?"

"There was a girl. I saw you turn her into a wild animal. I don't know what she did to wrong you, but no child deserves that. Turn her back. Let me take her home. I can look after her, help her find her family."

The witch stared at Annie Burton. Her expression was maddeningly blank. "That one you cannot have. Take your children and go, before I change my mind. Stay to your darling goblin's path, take nothing from my forest, and do not stray too near the bramble. Now, go."

Annie Burton saw two fluffy brown ears poke up from behind a fat log where they had been hiding. Hazel eyes and a wet black nose followed. Fable twitched a furry snout and mewled at the witch. Annie gave the girl a mournful glance before she turned to her boys.

"Wait. Where are they?" she said.

"Only sleeping," said the witch, gesturing behind her. "They will—" But then she, too, turned to look at the boys.

Tinn and Cole were gone.

"Where *are* they?" the queen demanded.

"Is this another test?" said Kull.

In the shadows of the Deep Dark, straining under the weight of a boy on either shoulder, Candlebeard ran.

TWENTY-ONE

TINN OPENED HIS EYES SLOWLY. THE WORLD sounded very far away, muffled and dim, as if he were viewing it not through his own eyes but through a long, foggy tunnel. As the haze gradually cleared, his senses came back into focus. All around him, the forest was gray and cold and unfamiliar. And then, abruptly, his vision was eclipsed by a face. He blinked. In front of him stood the strange little bearded man from the Oddmire, his expression a cluster of relief and panic and sadness and urgency all at once. Tinn began to feel dizzy just trying to take them all in.

He pushed himself up stiffly. Cole was seated a few feet away, looking equally groggy and rubbing his arm.

"Where are we?" asked Tinn.

"I don't know," Cole admitted.

"I had a dream . . ." Tinn hesitated. "I had a dream Mom came for us. But then we were . . . we were running." He shook his head. "Where are we? It's so dark."

"Watch out, there's thorns all over—" Cole began, but his warning came too late, and Tinn sliced his forearm on a nasty barb as he stretched.

"Ouch!" He pulled the arm back. The vine behind him was as thick as his leg, and the thorns were like bowie knives. All around them the forest seemed to have been overtaken by the nasty plants.

Across from Tinn, Cole winced. He held up his own arm, where a matching line of red had already been inscribed. "Got me, too."

"How did we get here?" said Tinn. "The last thing I remember is the queen."

Cole shrugged.

"Candlebeard?" said Tinn. "Did you—did you rescue us?"

The strange little man shuffled his feet. He nodded and then shook his head. His brow was wrinkled into a tortured knot and his lips were tight.

"He's probably embarrassed because he's the reason the

Queen of the Deep Dark caught us in the first place," said Cole.

Candlebeard looked as if he had swallowed a toad.

"Wait a minute—you didn't lead us to the witch on purpose, did you?"

Candlebeard shook his head *no*, but he didn't look any less wretched about it. From within his beard, his candle sputtered.

"It doesn't matter now," said Tinn. "He came back for us."

"Why *did* you come back for us?" said Cole.

The hinkypunk's shoulders drooped. He took a long, slow breath. When he was ready, he reached into the hollow of his beard. His weathered fingers passed right through the candle flame, and when he brought them out again, they were cupped as if holding a delicate butterfly. From his hands issued wisps of smoke.

Tinn and Cole watched in stunned silence as Candlebeard released his fingers. The little ball of smoke curled and dipped and spun as if it were alive. It slowed as it formed into foggy shapes. The boys leaned in, staring. From the living smoke emerged images—a silken vision of half a dozen bearded figures.

"The other hinkypunks," Tinn said. His breath scattered the vision and he closed his lips quickly.

Candlebeard gently scooped another puff of smoke into the dark clearing. It swam in midair until a new picture formed. Now there were just two larger figures standing over what appeared to be an infant. The figure on the left was very familiar.

"Is that you?" whispered Cole. "Did you have a little bearded baby?"

Candlebeard's eyes shone wetly and he sighed, lost in the memory. The delicate child of smoke lay still, its candle unlit. Above the infant, the cloudy vision of the hinkypunk reached into his beard and plucked out a smoky miniature candle. The figure across from him did the same. Tenderly, the two touched their flames together to light the third. They tucked the flickering candle into the infant's downy beard, and at once the baby's chest rose and fell, its tiny fingers wiggling.

The apparition was already beginning to dissipate into the darkness. Before it had faded completely, the boys watched the cloudy Candlebeard lift his child in his arms, his face alight with joy.

Candlebeard sat staring blankly at the empty air long after the images had vanished. Tears hung in the creased corners of his eyes.

"You looked very happy," Tinn said, breaking the silence.

Candlebeard nodded miserably.

"What happened to your son?" said Cole. "Was he taken away from you?"

Again, Candlebeard nodded. The tears rolled down his cheeks and nestled into his bristly mustache.

"That's why you came back for us, isn't it?" said Tinn. "You lost your child to the witch, and you didn't want her to take us, too."

Candlebeard's flame spat and flickered as the tears made their way down into his beard. He screwed his eyes shut and turned away.

"Thank you," said Cole.

Candlebeard shook his head and waved them off, batting away the gratitude. He sniffed and wiped his face on one arm, pulling himself together.

He gave the boys one more pained glance and, without further warning, began to wind his way between and through the labyrinth of inky black briars again.

"Wait, slow down," Cole said, jumping to his feet. He pushed himself up and darted after the hinkypunk.

The vines climbed higher and higher around them as Cole trailed behind Candlebeard, with Tinn following at his brother's heels. Shortly, they were not walking a trail at all, but crawling through spiral archways and claustrophobic tunnels of the pernicious plants. What little light made it through the brambles arrived sliced into thin ribbons. The flicker of Candlebeard's candle bobbed ahead of them farther and farther in the distance.

Fable was feeling a lot of things. She was feeling fur and paws and a tufty tail, yes, but she was also feeling guilty and worried and flustered.

A peculiar smell lingered in the air, and a part of Fable's mind kept telling her that it was important for some reason, but the rest of her mind was having trouble concentrating. Being an animal was very distracting. The grown-ups had not stopped arguing, which did not help.

"My fault?" The little angry man with all the sharp teeth was yelling at the witch. "Iffin you had just let us have the wee ones right off—but na! Had ta get all tricksy, an' now my changelin'—"

"Mind your tongue before I remove it, thief," the witch replied. "Who brought the changeling to the other side of the forest in the first place? Who left him there, a baby, unprotected, far from home, to be raised by strangers?"

Fable shook her head, trying to make sense of what they were talking about. Words sounded different through animal ears. Also, that smell kept tickling her nose, distracting her.

"Otch! Ya dinna have ta remind me, ya witchy womern! I'll be takin' the slippery blighter back fer good as quick as we can find him!"

Annie Burton jabbed a finger at the goblin. "Why, you—" And then she said several words that Fable was fairly certain she would not have been allowed to repeat as a human girl, even if she could remember them. "—and when we do find them, there is no way that I am ever letting you run away with either one of my children!" Annie concluded.

"Calm yerself," the goblin chided. "'Tis na like I'm stealin' yer own precious manling. I'm only takin' back the one what's not yorn."

"Spare us," huffed the queen. "You think we don't know what brought you into the baby's room all those years ago? Stealing her own true child was precisely your intention in the first place."

"Okay. Aye, that's a wee bit true. But . . . but I didn'a!" Kull protested weakly.

"Just because you weren't any good at being awful doesn't make you any less guilty."

Annie wheeled on the queen. "You," she barked, "do not get to help me. You steal children, too—and you turn them into . . . into things!"

Fable pushed the smell to the back of her animal mind and gave a growly sort of grumble. The adults were talking about her now, she could tell. She plodded forward on all fours while Annie railed at the queen.

"I saw you do it!" Annie continued. "There! That's her, right there—the poor girl." Annie was pointing right at Fable, who turned her shaggy head sideways at the woman. "Don't lie. You would have done the same to my boys if I hadn't stopped you! Admit it!"

"The girl is not your concern," said the queen.

"Of course she's my concern," said Annie. "She's an innocent child lost in the woods with a wicked witch. What sort of monster wouldn't be concerned?"

Fable stood on her hind legs beside the Queen of the Deep Dark. She still only came up to the witch's waist. She pawed pleadingly at the queen's cloak, her hazel eyes blinking their widest, sweetest, and saddest expression.

The queen turned her glare toward the girl, unmoved by her piteous appeal. "No," she said.

"Have you no heart at all?" Annie implored.

"'Course she doesn'a have a heart," Kull mumbled at Annie's back. "Na fer wee girlies lost in the Deep Dark."

The witch rolled her eyes. "Fine," she said at last, scowling down at the pitiful cub. "Go ahead."

Kull gaped.

Annie blinked. "Fine? You'll give her back her human body?"

"I will do no such thing. What I will give her," the queen said, still eyeing Fable, "is my permission."

Annie Burton blinked, not understanding. She glanced at Kull, but he only shrugged. When she turned back, Fable was a girl again.

"Hi," the girl said meekly.

"Oh! Goodness! Are you all right, sweetheart?" Annie asked.

"I— Wait a second . . ." Fable screwed up her eyebrows, concentrating. Thoughts were shuffling back into place in her human head. Yes, human brains definitely worked differently. She sniffed several times, turning this way and that.

"It's going to be okay," said Annie. "Do you know where you are right now?"

"Paraffin," said Fable, gazing into the trees.

"What?" asked Annie Burton.

The girl clutched at the witch's fur cloak. "It's candle wax! I can smell it! You know what that means!"

"You are wrong," said the queen. "Their kind have left the forest." But her nose twitched, and Fable could tell that she smelled it, too.

"They have not! I met one! How do you think I got so far into the Oddmire? Please, we need to hurry!"

"*We* need to do nothing of the sort. *You* aren't going anywhere until—"

The girl's voice was desperate. "They don't know the forest like I do!"

"*You* don't know the forest!"

"I know enough to know where they're headed."

The queen hesitated.

"Where are they headed?" Annie said, breathlessly. "What's going on?"

The queen's eyes flickered toward the trees for a moment.

"They might not know what's out that way, but *I* do," Fable said. "And you know it, too. You can't pretend you don't. Please. They'll die."

Annie's eyes bounced from the girl to the witch.

The queen regarded Fable coldly for a moment, then nodded. "Fine. Find them quickly," she said. "We will discuss your punishment after the boys are safe." Together, the girl and the witch started into the trees.

"Wait!" Annie called after them.

Fable turned, impatient. "Are you coming or what?"

"How can you just trust that woman to help you after what she did?" Annie asked. "Do you even know who she is—*what* she is?"

"Of course I do," said Fable. "She's my mom."

Mothers, fathers, daughters, sons. The words were meaningless to the Thing at the heart of the bramble. The Thing was born of *loneliness*. It had been raised with *fear* and *hate* for its only companions—these words it knew. *Family*, however? *Family* was a strange word. Family intrigued the creature.

At first, the notion had struck the Thing as utterly pointless. What purpose was there in a brother? What value in a sister? And then the creature had discovered it: *pain*.

In families there was *love*—a trivial, meaningless emotion, to be sure—but with *love* came *loss*. Loss was so much more exquisite than simple solitude. A happy family was dull to the Thing in the bramble. It was content and comfortable. When one tore a family apart, however, their pain would blossom. The suffering of a child ripped from its parent was misery tenfold anything the creature had known inside its perpetual prison, and it was delicious. The Thing had found a feast of torment in breaking apart families in its new forest home.

The fair folk had been especially delectable. The delight came from their magic, the Thing recalled fondly, the taste of their magic, the sensation of it filling the Thing's senses. It sighed. But then, gradually, the fair folk had left the Wild Wood. The Thing had been forced to satisfy itself with baby birds fallen from their nests, wolves

149

separated from their packs, a doe who had lost her fawn. A meager existence. Over the years, these, too, fell into its clutches less and less frequently. The Thing in the heart of the bramble was hungry.

A vine beneath it trembled. The Thing stiffened. The ragged cloak of shadows that defined the Thing's bulky form shivered in excitement. Something had been caught. The creature closed its eyes to feel its victim's panic rippling through the forest. A child. Good. Children were the best at fear.

A wave of energy snapped through the vine like an electric current, and the creature's eyes shot open. This was no fledgling fawn. The Thing's heart began to race. It had not felt power like this in a very long time.

The creature pulled its precious shadows closer, its nerves twitching in anticipation. It could feel the child's emotions pulsing at the other end of the vine—and it could feel the magic, real and raw, magic like the forest had all but forgotten. Tonight, the Thing at the heart of the bramble was going to feast.

TWENTY-TWO

"SHE'S REALLY YOUR CHILD?" ANNIE BURTON asked the queen as they pressed through the Deep Dark. Kull hung back nervously, twenty yards or so behind them, and Fable scurried twenty yards or so ahead. The girl moved through the forest like a fish through water. Annie moved through the forest more like a fish through—well— a forest, bumbling and stumbling over the uneven terrain every step of the way, but she managed to keep pace with the witch. "She's yours properly, I mean," she added. "You didn't steal her?"

Ahead of them, Fable vaulted over a fallen branch and then paused, pushing her thick curls out of her face to smell the breeze. Abruptly, she clenched her fists, closed her eyes, and held her breath—WHUMPH! She was a bear cub again, leaves spinning around her shaggy body.

Annie stared.

The cub dropped to the earth. She snuffled along the ground in front of her for a few paces and presently jumped up on her hind legs. In another flurry of movement, she was back to her human form.

Annie Burton shook her head in awed silence.

"This way!" Fable called out.

"Yes. She is mine," said the queen.

"So, you didn't turn her into an animal after all? She did that herself?"

"Fable has always been a precocious child."

Annie nodded. "And . . . her father?" she asked.

"Gone," said the queen in a tone that made it quite clear that branch of the conversation had reached its end.

Annie considered telling the woman about her own husband. About how her sweet Joseph had vanished shortly after their one baby became two babies, about how she had been left to raise them on her own without him. She hesitated. What was she thinking? Her husband was not a topic Annie Burton discussed with anyone—least of all a sinister sorceress who would as happily steal her children as save them.

"Who are you, really?" Annie said, instead.

"I am the Witch of the Wood," the woman answered, flatly. "I'm sure you've heard the titles. Queen of—"

"But are you, actually? Are you the witch from the stories? Do you blight crops and transform into horrible monsters and eat children?"

The queen eyed Annie. "Somebody has to," she said, shrugging. "Crops don't just blight themselves, after all." A hint of a smile teased at the corner of the witch's lip. "But you doubt the stories, I can tell. What did you say your name was?"

"Annie Burton."

"Tell me, Annie Burton, did you ever believe them? When you were young, did you believe that the Queen of the Deep Dark would gobble you up if you trod too far into the Wild Wood?"

Annie swallowed, and decided to be honest. "Yes. When I was young."

"And did the stories keep you from treading too far into the wood?"

Annie considered. "I suppose so."

The queen's grin was wicked, but also somehow warm. "I love those stories. They are my stories. And they serve their purpose."

A squat boulder blocked their path, and the queen stepped over it as smoothly as if it were a lumpy cobblestone.

The forest seemed to bend around the will of the witch, as though it really were bowing to its queen. Annie had to use both hands to scramble over the thing, and a creeping briar tore the hem of her skirt as she slid down the opposite side. She would have to mend that later. For half a second she marveled at the thought of ever again doing something as ordinary as sewing, and then she jogged to catch up to the wicked witch in the middle of the Deep Dark.

"But are they true?" she panted. "The stories about you capturing lost boys and girls? Is that why you don't age? Is it something to do with stealing children's youth or something?"

The queen raised an eyebrow. At length she said: "I age."

"Then how can you be her? You're much too young. You don't look much older than I am. We told stories about an old witch when I was just a child—so you can't be the same witch, not after all this time."

The Queen of the Deep Dark shook her head, amused. "Just because a story is not yours to begin does not mean it isn't yours to finish. Just because it isn't yours to finish does not mean it isn't yours to begin."

"Oh," said Annie. And then: "Sorry, what does that mean?"

With a sigh, the queen put her hand out and brushed

154

the trunk of a broad pine tree. "Let's try it another way," she said. "I did not plant this tree. It was here long before me, and it will still be here long after I am gone. Am I important to the tree?"

"No?"

"What if a woodsman came into the forest with an ax and I chased him away from the tree? Would I have been important to it then?"

"Well, yes, obviously."

"What if I teach my little Fable how to chase the woodsmen off, and Fable teaches her children, and so on—will I have been important to the tree then?"

Annie nodded.

"That is how stories work. Stories are important. They are born, they die, they're born again—but while they live they chase away the woodsmen that threaten their trees."

"That's a lovely sentiment," Annie said, "but I'm afraid you've lost me. Are you talking about you or about stories?"

"Yes," said the queen.

Ahead of them, Fable had transformed into a bear cub once more and was turning in circles as she sniffed the earth. For several seconds the two women stood in silence and watched her.

"I . . . I think I understand," Annie said softly.

"Do you?"

"I don't think you're terrible at all."

The queen said nothing.

"I think they're all just stories," Annie said. "Stories to protect children from the forest."

The witch's hard laugh startled Annie.

"No?" Annie said.

"It is not my task to protect your idiot children from my forest, Annie Burton. I protect my forest."

"From . . . children?"

"From what children become."

Up ahead, Fable appeared to have caught the scent again at last, and she hurried onward through the bracken.

The queen did not rush after her at once. Something about the way she was looking at Annie made the old, scary stories feel plausible, indeed.

"This is my forest," said the queen, "my trees, my beasts, my monsters. They are my children to protect. When the woodsmen come with their axes, well . . ." Her eyes narrowed as she let the sentence trail off. "You would do well, Annie Burton, never to underestimate just how *terrible* I can be."

Before Annie could find the words to respond, Fable's voice cut through the trees ahead. "Ouch! Ow! Let me go! LET GO!"

The queen's eyes flashed like fire. In one fluid motion

she leapt forward and pulled the furry hood over her head. The cloak swelled, the forest trembled, and Annie Burton found herself staring up at a massive grizzly bear. The creature's lips curled into a grotesque sneer as she growled, deep and rumbling.

A moment later, her front paws slammed into the ground and the beast thundered off into the forest toward the sound of Fable's cries. With an effortless swipe, she cleaved a bush in two.

Annie's heart thudded. Her life had turned into madness. That morning she had wanted nothing more than a cup of tea, and now there were real goblins and sinister swamps and strange women who turned into bears—and her boys were still gone. Her morning felt worlds away. A part of her was terrified. A part of her wanted to run away, run back home to a fat old house cat and piles of laundry and lukewarm tea—but a different part of her kept pressing against her rib cage. It pulled her forward, into the dark. The sound the bear was making just beyond the bushes was the stuff of nightmares, but Annie recognized that growl on another level. That growl was the sound her heart made when her boys needed her most. Her boys needed her now, just as Fable needed the witch.

Annie took a deep breath as she prepared to follow the bear-queen into the darkness. The deafening crunch of a tree cracking and crashing to the ground echoed through the woods before she could even take her first step. Birds erupted from the leaves all around her, fleeing for quieter skies. Total chaos was erupting from the forest ahead.

"That's why I dinna stand in front," said Kull, plodding past. "Come on."

TWENTY-THREE

TINN COULD BARELY SEE THE THIN, PRICKLY VINE that looped around his ankle in the gloom. As he reached down to free himself from it, a tiny barb greedily bit his thumb. He sucked on the injury, and the coppery taste of the blood mixed with the earthy grime and dust of his journey. Ahead of him, Cole pulled back his own hand as another thorn caught him in the same thumb. The boys pushed forward. All things considered, a cut was nothing— they were lucky they hadn't already been carved to tatters in the dense maze of thorns as they did their best to keep up with Candlebeard.

The whole thing felt wrong to the pit of Tinn's stomach.

It was more than the darkness, more than the pain. The vines were moving—bending and creeping like living snakes as the boys traveled beneath them, the path opening ever so slightly ahead of them, closing ever so stealthily behind them.

Cole stopped, and Tinn drew up beside him.

"What's wrong?"

"I can't find the path," said Cole. He was straining his eyes, feeling his way around, but in every direction he could find only more brambles.

Up ahead, they could see the hinkypunk's light flickering weakly behind layers and layers of the dense vines.

"Candlebeard!" Cole called. "Come back, we're stuck!"

The candlelight neared, and they could just barely make out the old man's face beyond the wall of thorns. "I'm so sorry," he whispered. His voice was dry and cracked like broken chalk.

"You talk?" Tinn said.

"Don't do this," said Cole, tugging fruitlessly at the vines. "You came back for us! Please don't do this!"

"Don't do what? What's he doing?" Tinn said. He looked from Cole to Candlebeard. "How do we get out, Candlebeard?"

"I'm so sorry. I'm so sorry. I'm so sorry." Candlebeard was crying now, shaking his head.

"Candlebeard, you get us out of here right now!" Cole yelled, but the vines were already slithering into a dense mesh, squeezing tighter and tighter together, until every inch of the hinkypunk's miserable face had been hidden from view. "Aaaaaargh!" Cole yelled, tearing at the vicious things. He succeeded only in carving a deep gash in his palm.

Tinn just stood, frozen. "He—he left us."

"He lied to us!" Cole yelled through the inscrutable wall. "He's a dirty, rotten monster, and he lied to us all along!"

Ever so slowly, like the last trickle of maple syrup slowly running off the spoon, the faltering beams of sunlight faded away completely and the world went black.

Fable screamed again. Wicked black barbs had wrapped themselves around both ankles now, and the harder the girl kicked and thrashed, the more fiercely they bit into her legs. She fell backward onto the cold ground. With both hands she tried to pull herself away from the plant, but the vines pulled back.

She hadn't even seen them at first, so heavy were the shadows in the Deep Dark. She had only been paying attention to the scent—paraffin, sharp and faintly sweet, the unmistakable trail of the hinkypunk's candle. It had been so fresh and close, she could imagine Candlebeard waiting just over the next hill with Cole and Tinn. She had allowed her eager hope to cloud her caution, and by the time she had realized her mistake she was already up to her knees in the awful vines. The bramble had waited for her to try to turn back before it closed in and snared her with its biting thorns.

The forest behind her rustled and she heard her mother's roar. Moonlight cut through the forest canopy like a spear, and Fable could see clearly the vines that had trapped her. They were writhing like a mess of vipers, clambering to overtake her, long tendrils reaching out of a massive mountain of thorns.

In another instant, Fable's mother was looming over her, beastly muscles rippling under heavy fur and dark lips curling back over monstrous fangs. Fable breathed a sigh of relief.

The great bear tore at the vines holding Fable's feet. Fable felt her legs yanked up and down with each swipe. The beast's long talons should have carved easily through the cords, but blow after blow, they held fast. The queen barked with pain and fury, but she did not relent. Fable could see blood on her mother's paws.

The bramble shuddered and swelled in the dim light. Fable watched in horror as a new wave of dark vines bulged forward, rolling toward them from the main bulk. Her mother fell back. Fable clawed at the ground, trying to get away before she was buried beneath the oncoming cascade, but she found nothing to grip but damp, slippery leaves.

She heard a sharp crunch and a snap of wood splintering to her left just as the wave of thorns swelled in front of her. And then a deafening CRACK echoed through the forest, and a mossy tree trunk thicker around than Fable herself came crashing down on top of the slithering brambles. Her mother had thrown an entire tree at the vicious vines.

The painful pressure around Fable's ankles loosened. She pulled her foot back experimentally. The vines tried to hold her, but crushed as they were under the weight of the trunk, they had lost most of their strength. Fable was twisting her feet this way and that to slide them free when she felt a sudden grip on her wrist. Startled, she wrenched her arm away.

"It's me," said a familiar voice. She blinked up at Annie Burton. "Take my hand," Annie urged. "Come on!"

Fable took Annie's hands in hers and kicked at the vines as the woman pulled. They sliced at her legs angrily, but she ignored the pain.

"It's na good," grumbled the goblin from somewhere behind them. "They dinna let go until they's satisfied."

"You could help us, you cretin," Annie barked over her shoulder, kicking at the creeping plants as she kept a firm grip on Fable.

Inky black tendrils were beginning to peek over the top of the fallen tree. It would not take the bramble long to overcome the obstacle. Fable felt the ground shudder as her mother bounded atop it to swipe at the nasty things.

"Ya'll na see me gettin' that close," Kull called back. "Even if the bramble lets the wee witchy free, it'll just take another in her place."

"I suppose you'd rather just let it have her?" Annie demanded.

"It's na havin' me."

"Ugh," Annie grunted in disgust.

"Please don't let it take me," Fable squeaked.

"I'm not letting go, sweetheart," Annie promised, redoubling her efforts.

Fable's legs felt like they were on fire, but with a final effort she wrenched one foot free and then the other. Together, she and Annie tumbled backward into the bracken.

Fable gasped, panting, and pushed herself to sitting. For one terrifying moment, she couldn't see her mother. Where was she? She had been atop the tree trunk only a moment ago. Dread crept into Fable's mind. Had the bramble taken her mother in Fable's place?

And then the ground shook as the bear landed hard beside them. The big beast's hot breath blew Fable's curls around on her forehead, and Fable smiled. The bear grunted. Her muscles quivered and she slumped to the ground, panting. Her shoulders rose and fell, her whole body shuddering until the bear was gone and the queen was a woman once again, panting heavily beneath her heavy fur cloak.

Fable turned her eyes warily back to the bramble. The tendrils pinched beneath the tree remained where they had been trapped, as lifeless and still as if they had never been anything more than harmless forest foliage.

"It's stopped," Fable whispered.

"That's na good," said Kull.

"Not good?" Annie huffed. "We're exceedingly lucky that we all came out of that alive, no thanks to you."

"Aye, 'tis luck, but na the good kind. This is bad. Very bad. The wee witchy didn'a satisfy the bramble."

"What, and you *wanted* her to? You are a horrible, vile—"

"No." The queen cut her off, her voice strained. A line of deep crimson had cut down her cheek, and she drew her breath through clenched teeth. "The thief is right. Look." The swell of vines that had been crawling over the fallen tree had retreated, ebbing back to melt into the dark mass in the shadowy center of the forest. The bramble fell dormant and docile. "It's quiet, and we're all still here," the queen said. "That's not how the bramble works. If Fable did not satisfy it, then something else did."

"Ya see, womern? That's what I've been trying to—"

"You repugnant man, stop talking." The queen's eyes met Annie's.

Annie felt her heart lurch. The queen did not need to say it aloud—Annie knew what she was thinking. "We don't know that it has my boys," she said. Her voice cracked, and she cleared her throat.

The queen let her eyes drop, and for some reason that made it worse.

Annie shook her head. "We don't know that," she repeated with forced conviction. "Come here, Fable. Let me put something on those cuts."

"Wait," said the queen, wincing as she pushed herself up. Without further explanation, she staggered off into the trees.

"Where are you going?" Annie said.

"Wait," came the witch's voice.

Kull shrugged.

Annie was not about to sit idle until the insufferable woman reappeared. She tore long strips from the hem of her skirt, doing her best to keep her hands from shaking as she fashioned crude bandages for the girl's bloody ankles. There was little she could do to clean or treat them here in the middle of the forest, but she could cover them, at least.

She was ready to begin wrapping when the queen returned and dropped a sticky golden lump into her lap and then slid down against the base of a tree.

"Ugh! What on earth?"

"Honeycomb. For the pain, and to help her to heal more quickly."

"Oh." Annie's grandmother had sworn by honey for cuts. "Right. Okay." She ran her hand along the comb to scoop out as much honey as she could. Gingerly, she daubed it on the worst of Fable's injuries. Fable bit her lip and winced, but she did not allow herself to cry.

"Annie Burton," said the queen. Annie glanced up. The queen was breathing heavily, but a little color seemed to be coming back to her cheeks as she rested. "Thank you."

Annie nodded. She finished with the last of the honey and then did her best to clean her hands off on her skirt before applying the bandages.

"I suppose there's still hope," Kull mused aloud. "Maybe that wicked weed only got yer manling and na my changelin', too."

Annie looked up from her work long enough to stare daggers at the goblin.

"Oi—dinna gimme that look, womern. Isn'a like I *want* any of the wee ones dead. More at stake, is all. If ya want to look at someone all angry like, look at her!" He jabbed a thumb toward the queen. "Wouldn'a be a problem iffin our witchy here had na planted the devil itself for her garden hedge."

"That bramble is not my doing," the queen growled. "It is not of these woods. It is an unnatural, invasive thing. If I had recognized the pernicious plant when it was small, I would have plucked it out by its roots and burned it long ago. I have failed in my charge—allowed it to grow for far too long. It creeps farther when it is hungry and grows stronger when it is fed. I cannot control it. And the thief is right. When it has a victim in its grasp, it is relentless until satisfied."

"If the bramble needs a sacrifice in place of my children, I'm more than happy to let you toss this miscreant in." Annie glared at Kull.

"Oi. That's na very fair now, is it?"

"Fair? The baby-stealing, child-sacrificing goblin really wants to talk about what's fair?" Annie tied off the last bandage. Fable stretched her legs and wiggled her feet experimentally.

"Goblins is fair," Kull said, hotly. "Goblins is always fair. Goblins has rules."

"I suppose your rules abide abducting innocent children from their beds in the middle of the night?"

"Otch! It's na goblins' fault. It's the fairies who wants the wee babies, na goblins—goblins is just better at sneakin'. The fairies is the guilty parties. Goblins make sure o' it. We put it in the contract. Fairies buy the babies *and* all the responsibility from us—fer a reasonable price."

The queen took to her feet in one fluid movement. She rose until she was towering in front of Kull, the ends of her tattered cloak swaying around her feet. Kull looked up. The queen looked down. The goblin's throat suddenly felt dry.

"How much?" the witch said coldly.

"How much?"

"You say you sold children to the fair folk for a *reasonable price*. How much?"

"Thinkin' o' gettin' into the baby-sellin' business?" Kull nodded with a weak smile. "From the stories I hear, ya'd be a fair hand at it, hag. Depends entirely on the buyer, of course, and the baby and—"

"How much," the witch said slowly, "did you get . . . for *me*?"

For several very uncomfortable moments, Kull opened and closed his mouth without achieving actual speech. The queen's eyes narrowed. She did not look away.

Fable looked from her mother to the goblin and back again. Her mother had never spoken about any of this to Fable.

"You—you were the girl," said Annie at last. "You weren't the witch from the stories at all, you were the little girl, the one with dimples and thick brown curls. You were the last child the goblins stole away, weren't you?"

The queen stared at Annie for a long time, her brow low and her eyes as black as the forest around her. Without answering, she turned to Fable. The girl's expression was wide-eyed and wondering.

"Can you walk?" the queen asked flatly.

Fable stood cautiously, testing out her legs. The bandages Annie had wrapped around them were snug but not too tight. They did not completely erase the pain, but they shielded her injuries from the bite of the cold air. She nodded.

The queen spun, her bearskin cloak sweeping across the face of the speechless goblin. "We have stalled for long enough," she said, pressing on up a forest path that wound around the bramble.

"That was so long ago," Annie said. "What happened to you?"

The Queen of the Deep Dark did not turn to face her. "We will find your children, Annie Burton," she said.

TWENTY-FOUR

THE ONLY SOUND WITHIN THE TWINS' THORNY
prison was the scratch of a matchstick along the side of its
box. Then silence. Darkness. Another scratch. For a brief
moment, the flash of a spark lit up Tinn's shaking hands.
He nearly dropped the matchbox.

It was soaked through from his tumble into the mire,
but if only he could coax it to light . . . *Scratch. Scratch.*
Scratch.

At last, a sputtering flame flared up. Almost at once it
faded to nearly nothing, but Tinn cupped his hand around
it and held the weak, stuttering light perfectly still. He held
his breath. After several seconds, the tiny fire grew by a

fraction and began to crawl grudgingly up the matchstick. He rattled the little box with his other hand. Three left.

"Good job," said Cole. "Hey. Over here. I think I see a path."

"Are you sure?" Tinn strained his eyes. An almost perfect dome of vines surrounded them now, so the meager matchlight glistened off sharp thorns in every direction. The path beyond Cole was the only opening.

"It's either go this way or stay here until we run out of matches," Cole said. "It's okay. I'll go first. Hold the light up over my shoulder."

The boys crept deeper into the bramble, their backs hunched under the canopy of vines. Cole led slowly, testing each cautious step before moving forward. The tunnel twisted and curved, so it was never possible to see more than a few feet ahead or behind. Tinn kept close, holding the light as high as he could. The fire burned his fingers before he finally let the match fall, dwindled to twisted ash, on the forest floor.

Scratch. Scratch. Scratch. The next match lit on the third strike, and the boys pressed forward again. The bramble grew denser. It was not long before Cole had dropped to his knees to crawl under the shrinking tunnel.

Tinn lost his footing almost at once. The ground was unsteady through this narrow corridor, covered in thick roots and pale branches. Tinn's free hand darted out to catch his fall, and his hand landed directly on one of the wicked thorns, carving a deep gash across his palm.

He hissed through his teeth, but managed to keep the match aloft. Until they were free from the bramble, there was nothing to be done. Tinn had already seen Cole suffer the same injury. Cole hadn't cried, so Tinn would not cry. He would just focus on keeping his balance and ignore the pain until it dulled.

"Where do you think it leads?" Tinn whispered, trying hard to keep the flickering light above his brother.

"Out," grunted Cole, hoping that his voice sounded more optimistic than he felt. Cole's heart pounded heavily against his ribs. Each beat pulsed sharply in the cut on his own palm.

The light bobbing over Cole's shoulder lit up the ground in uneven patches. The knobby, broken branches beneath his fingers felt cold and dry and wrong, not like wood at all.

Slowly, carefully, he picked one up. The branch was more than just pale, it was ivory white. And it wasn't a branch.

Cole turned to face Tinn. He swallowed.

"Is that a . . ." Tinn whispered.

Cole nodded. Tinn lowered the matchstick. As one, the boys looked down at the ground beneath them.

Bones. Large and small, broken and whole, some as long as the boys were tall, some no larger than a fingernail clipping—the ground was carpeted with the bones of countless creatures. Victims.

A wave of cold swept through the black corridor.

The match in Tinn's hand flickered out.

TWENTY-FIVE

IT WAS TIME AT LAST. THE THING BREATHED IN
deeply. There would be no escape for the children, not
now. With every step, they moved only farther into its nest.
The Thing could take its time. There were two of them. So
alike and different at once. Their fear, their misery, their
panic and distress—the Thing could taste the sweet emotions through every prick of the ebony thorns.

But then there was the magic.

The Thing moaned in anticipation. Raw, ripe, mouth-
watering magic coursed through one of the boys—more
magic than any paltry spriggan or gnome or hinkypunk.

Magic, raw and pure and powerful, waiting just under his skin. Goblin? More than goblin. A changeling. The Thing closed in on the boys. It would eat the human first and save the exquisite changeling for last.

TWENTY-SIX

SCRATCH. SCRATCH. SCRATCH. TINN'S THIRD matchstick finally burst to life. "One left," he breathed.

"We're getting out of here," said Cole. He could see the despair in his brother's eyes.

"We're only getting deeper," said Tinn.

Cole pulled out his pocketknife. "I promise." With all his strength he carved at the vines. They bowed and swayed under the pressure, but he might as well have been trying to carve through iron chains.

Tinn sighed. The matchstick was already nearly spent.

Cole closed the blade with a huff and stuffed the knife back into his pocket. He picked up a long bone. It was as

177

thick as his wrist and ended in a knobbly Y on one end. He pushed the bone against the branches as hard as he could. In response, the wall pressed back a foot or so, forming a shallow alcove. Cole shoved the bone against the ground to wedge it in place, and when he let go, it held its position.

"Huh," said Cole. So they couldn't cut their way out of the vines, but maybe they could push them aside.

Tinn hastened to help, picking out more strong bones with his free hand to pass to his brother. Propping bones in place one by one, Cole gained another two feet, then three feet, four feet. Painstakingly, they were leaving the bramble's sinister path and forging their own. For the first time since Candlebeard had left them there, Tinn felt actual hope. And then the matchstick faded out.

Scratch. Scratch. Scratch. While Tinn tried furiously to get the final match to ignite, Cole groped blindly for another sturdy bone to brace against the barbs. His fingers sifted through thin, fragile, fragmented remains until they wrapped around something soft and waxy. It was small enough to fit in his palm, and he was about to toss it aside when the match beside him finally caught.

Tinn tucked the matchbox away and protected the flame with his hand. He glanced around. The path the bramble wanted them to take appeared much wider and taller than their makeshift tunnel by the light of their final match—it looked downright inviting, if it weren't for the carpet of bones that lined it. Tinn shuddered. He looked at Cole. Cole was looking at the object in his hand. It was pale and pearly, but it was not another bone—it was a candle stub.

The two of them stared for a moment, and then the match fluttered, and Tinn tilted it to keep the paltry fire alive.

"Hold it still," said Cole. He leaned forward. The flame licked the candle's wick, but it would not catch. "Come on. Come on."

They turned the candle this way and that, willing the wick to light, but it was no use. Soon the final match was nearly spent, its precious light wasted on the unwilling wick. The candle might as well have been made of stone for all the good it had done them.

"Argh," Cole growled. "Forget it! It's not working!" He stuffed the candle stub into his pocket and stomped back to scan the floor for sturdy bones.

"It's our last match," said Tinn. "Cole?" The light flickered. It dimmed.

A pair of antlers was half buried in the gloom ahead of Cole, and he tugged on them, trying to free them from the other relics.

"Cole?" Tinn repeated. And then the light died. Once more shrouded in darkness, Tinn finally let himself cry.

He could hear his brother working still, pulling at the antlers, wrestling with the thorny vines in the darkness. For once, Tinn wanted to be the brave one. He wanted to save the day. He wanted to fix this. Tears fell hot on his cheeks.

Just when he thought he could not possibly feel worse, an unnatural cold crept over him. This was worse than the wet Oddmire, worse than a winter wind. This cold was absolute. It crept all around him, soaked through him. The hairs along Tinn's arms stood on end. The world was ice and darkness, punctuated only by hollow echoes. He could hear his own heart thudding. He could hear Cole panting and struggling right in front of him.

And he could hear something moving through the bramble right behind them.

TWENTY-SEVEN

THE THING SLIPPED THROUGH THE VINES, ITS cloak of shadows billowing behind it, unhindered by the thorny barbs. The boys were just ahead now—the human and the changeling.

The Thing swelled and solidified as it closed in on them. It was roughly human now, if only a carnival-mirror reflection of its latest victims, draped as always in its cloak of tattered shadows. The Thing grew until its shoulders brushed the thorny canopy above it. The larger it grew, the hungrier it felt. It had been so long since the creature had fed, really fed.

The Thing's unwilling servants brought him scraps from time to time, barely enough to sustain it. And, of course, when their offerings dwindled, the Thing just fed on the servants instead—not that they were much better fare. The children, though, these tasty morsels ensnared within its vines, these were different. The magic of the changeling hummed through the entire bramble, and the creature's mouth watered.

It moved closer still until it could see the boys through the web of briars. They struggled blindly, helplessly. The Thing smiled. Did they know they were about to die? The Thing liked it when they knew.

TWENTY-EIGHT

Tinn's heart felt like ice. Something was definitely moving just beyond the vines. Was that the sound of fabric catching on thorns? Talons scraping bones? He couldn't tell.

His eyes watered as he strained to make out anything at all in the direction of the noise. And then all at once a shaft of pure white light cut through the gloom.

Tinn whirled around. Cole whooped.

"Sunlight!" Cole yelled. "Tinn! We're getting out of here!"

Cole pushed forward with abandon now, the thorns slicing mercilessly through his shirtsleeves, but he did not care. He barely felt the cuts anymore—soon he would be free.

Tinn glanced back at the vines behind him. In the beam of sunlight, he thought for just a moment that he saw motion within the inky blackness of the bramble. A feeling deep in his belly told him not to turn his back on that patch of darkness. He placed a hand on the vines, pressing them away to peer into the shadows.

A wave of unnatural cold washed over Tinn again, and the feeling weighed on him like heavy chains. The hair on the back of his neck stood on end and every nerve was screaming, but still he could not bring himself to look away. The horrible *something* was there. It was right there—right in front of him. He knew it, but he could not see it. He could not move. He could not breathe.

With every ounce of will left in him, Tinn wished that he were invisible. He wished that he could fade away to nothing and that the monster in the darkness would look right past him and go away. His fingers tingled. It was a familiar dread, but magnified tenfold. Tinn had wished himself invisible countless times. He had wished himself invisible every time Cole had convinced him to cut through the quarry or climb the water tower or sneak into Old Jim's orchard. It was not the first time Tinn had wished to be invisible—but it was the first time that it worked.

Tinn blinked. His fingers were suddenly midnight black against the vines. His whole hand had turned into the purest ink. He glanced down. More than just black in color, his entire chest had taken on the texture of the dark, braided vines.

Before Tinn's reeling mind could make sense of what was happening, the Thing slid out of the vines and stood beside him. It rippled and swelled as it emerged from the wall of thorns, its tattered black cloak sliding like liquid over the terrible barbs as though they weren't even there. The creature from the bramble hesitated not more than a foot from Tinn, radiating raw, wretched cold. It cocked its head ever so slightly, listening. Tinn's head spun.

Behind him, completely unaware, Cole burst at last into the fresh air of the forest. He laughed. "Ha! I'm through! Tinn, I'm through! I told you we were getting out of here! Come on!" Cole had not seen Tinn change. He had not seen the Thing arrive.

Tinn did not dare breathe. They had known going into the woods that only one of them would be coming back. They hadn't talked about it, but they knew that only one of them would wake up in bed the following morning, only one would go to school again in the fall, only one would dance nervously with a girl in the spring. Only one of them had a life waiting for him outside the Wild Wood. Only one of them was a real boy.

Tinn looked down at his hands. His fingers were inky vines. His skin was made of rippling shadows. He looked up into the light at the end of the barbed tunnel, where his brother was breathing fresh air. Only one of them had a mother and a home to return to. Only one of them had a chance.

And it wasn't Tinn.

The Thing breathed deeply. The human child had clawed its way free of the vines. Let the child flee; the human was nothing now. Where was the changeling?

"Tinn?" the human child called into the bramble. Was the fool coming back? "Tinn?"

So, the changeling was called *Tinn*. The Thing turned its head this way and that, searching. Tinn had not escaped its bramble, the Thing was sure of it. It could still sense him somewhere close, numb with fear and cold. Yet the Thing could not see him. Very well. The Thing would devour the human first, after all. It would let the changeling watch.

"Come on, Tinn! What are you waiting for?"

The Thing began to slink toward the sound of Cole's voice.

"Don't be afraid," Cole called, oblivious to the creature slipping closer to him in the shadows. "You can make it, Tinn. Just follow me!"

Tinn's heart hurt. His pulse boomed in his ears, and his breaths rose fast in his chest. All he had ever wanted his whole life had been to follow Cole—he would have followed Cole to the ends of the Earth.

"Do you need me to come back in there and get you?" Cole asked. He began to work his shoulders back through the vicious vines, blinking blindly into the pitch darkness. "Tinn?" The Thing's cloak of shadows quivered as it prepared to strike its target.

The twins had run out of time. A strange calm fell over Tinn. All the time in the world could not save him now. But it could save Cole.

Tinn tensed. When he moved, he moved very quickly.

There were a dozen bones wedged in the gap, holding Cole's narrow passage open. Tinn threw himself between them and shoved Cole's face back out of the bramble.

Cole gasped in surprise as the cold, dark fingers forced

him back. A face like carved obsidian appeared within the vines, alien, and yet familiar.

"Take care of Mom," Tinn said. Then he grabbed hold of the longest bone, the one right at the center of the tunnel, and pulled it free, knocking down the rest of them with it as he withdrew back into the bramble.

The vines collapsed into themselves in a rush, devouring the gap and snapping out the light like a snuffed lantern. Tinn threw himself backward and felt the wave of cold sweep over him.

TWENTY-NINE

"TINN!" COLE SCREAMED. HE TORE AT THE VINES with his bare hands until his arms were covered with deep, angry cuts. The gap would not reopen. He raged and thrashed and pulled at the unyielding bramble until the world spun around him and he collapsed to his knees. His sleeves were shredded to ribbons and with every heartbeat his arms throbbed as if they were on fire. "Tinn," he whimpered.

"I'm so sorry," said a meek voice behind him. "I'm so sorry."

Cole started and spun. Candlebeard was there, between two mossy trees.

"YOU!" Cole grabbed a handful of loose rocks and hurled them at the wretched hinkypunk. "You did this! You're a liar! Get away from me!"

"Didn't lie," Candlebeard mumbled to the ground. "Can't lie. Only speak the truth. I'm so sorry. I'm so, so sorry."

"Stop saying that! You tricked us! You gave us to that—that *whatever*. You fed my brother to a monster! *You're* a monster! I'm supposed to care that you're sorry? If you're so sorry, GET HIM BACK!"

Candlebeard's back hunched so low that his beard curled up where it pressed against the earth.

Cole panted, his anger thudding in his ears with every heartbeat. "WHY?" he demanded. "Why did you do it? What did we ever do to you? What did Tinn ever do to you?"

Fat, wet tears fell from Candlebeard's face. He reached into his chest and produced another ball of smoke, which he sculpted into the image of the bearded infant he had shown them earlier. "My son," he croaked.

Cole's rage caught in his throat. He wanted to rail against the treacherous man, but the pathetic figure slumped before him already looked completely defeated. Exhausted and bleeding, Cole sat in a heap on the cold ground. This wasn't how adventures were supposed to end.

The smoky apparition in Candlebeard's trembling hands spun slowly around. "My son," he breathed. Climbing tendrils of smoke clutched the wispy image of the boy. The terrified face of the hinkypunk child hung translucent in the air for a few seconds as vaporous vines consumed it. Candlebeard dropped his arms, his shoulders shaking.

Cole stared at the fading smoke. "It wasn't the queen that took your kid. It was that thing in the thorns, wasn't it? It still has him?"

Candlebeard nodded.

"Is that why you couldn't leave with the rest of your people?"

He nodded again. "It makes me do things." The old man sniffled. "Never enough. Never satisfied. Wants your brother. Your brother for my son. I'm so sorry. So, so, so sorry."

Tears dripped into Candlebeard's flame and sizzled.

At the mention of Tinn, Cole felt his cheeks grow hot. His fury was wasted on the broken old man, but it still simmered inside him. "Quit blubbering," he said. "You'll put your candle out."

Candlebeard shook his head. "Only at the end of me," he mumbled. "My candle. My life."

Cole narrowed his eyes, watching the old man weep.

"Let it go out." Candlebeard sniffled.

191

A dull, heavy realization settled over Cole. "Giving up my brother won't get your son back," he said heavily. He reached into his pocket. "I don't think anything will."

Candlebeard wiped his face along one arm and lifted his head. And then he saw what Cole was holding.

Tenderly, delicately, he took the candle stub in both hands as if it were a soap bubble and might burst at any moment.

"Is it . . . ?" Cole couldn't finish the question. The look on Candlebeard's face told him that it was. "We found it in the thorns."

Candlebeard's whole body shook. "So much wasted," he said. "So much left. My son. My light."

"I'm sorry," said Cole. "I wish that I could help you, but it's not too late for you to help me. You owe me that much. We can still save my brother."

Candlebeard's eyes were squeezed shut. "Killed him," he rasped. "Told me if I did those awful things . . . but then it killed him."

"And it's trying to kill Tinn, too," Cole pressed. "Please! How can I get back inside the bramble?"

"He would be so ashamed of the things I've done." Candlebeard couldn't seem to hear a word Cole was saying. "He would be so ashamed to have me for a father."

"Please, Candlebeard. Look, I never even knew my dad! My dad ran away because of what I *might* have been. He never came back for me. I wasn't worth coming back for, I guess."

Candlebeard stopped mumbling for a moment, although his head still hung at his chest.

"At least you never gave up on your son," Cole pressed. "You did things that were wrong, but it's never too late to do something right. It's not too late to do something he would be proud of."

The hinkypunk's eyes flashed open, rimmed with red, damp with tears, but alive with something Cole had not seen in them before. The fire in his chest flared as if someone had turned up an oil lamp. When the hinkypunk spoke again, it was through gritted teeth. "My son."

And then the strange little man leapt between the trees and vanished into the forest.

"Wait!" Cole pushed himself to his feet. He nearly toppled over again from the effort, but he managed to stagger toward the trees. Candlebeard was gone. "Argh!"

Cole sat down at the base of the tree, utterly alone. His arms and legs stung, but the pain was like someone else's now. He wanted his brother back. He wanted his mother. He wanted to go home. A noise in the brush beside him made him jump. He braced himself. What else was this nightmare forest going to throw at him? Wolves? Ogres? Giants?

Out of the foliage toddled a fluffy bear cub. Cole wiped his nose on the back of his ragged sleeve. The cub looked at Cole and pushed itself up on its wobbly hind legs, taking a few uncertain steps closer.

"Oh, no you don't," Cole told it. "Get! Shoo! The last time we helped you out, your mother nearly took my face off!"

The cub reached out a paw. It had something clutched between its sharp claws. Cole blinked. The cub was holding a marmalade tart.

"That's . . . uh . . ." Cole didn't know how to finish his sentence.

The cub ducked its head and turned away, and in a sudden *whumph* it had changed. "I lied to you," said Fable, looking down and wiggling her human toes in the dirt. "There was one more left. It was in my pocket all along. I just didn't want to share."

Behind her, the bushes rustled once more, and this time the Queen of the Deep Dark emerged from the shadows. Cole gaped and pushed back clumsily from her. The witch put a hand on Fable's shoulder and addressed Cole gently. "Hello again, child," she said. "I promise I have no intention of taking your face off. This time."

And then the leaves exploded outward as one last figure burst into the clearing. Cole's throat tightened and his eyes stung as he stared in disbelief. Then his mother's arms were tight around him and his were around her and they were both lying on the dirty ground crying.

Fable beamed as she stuffed the last marmalade tart in her mouth.

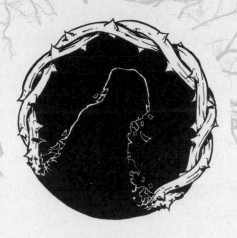

THIRTY

Tɪɴɴ ʟᴀʏ ᴡɪᴛʜ ʜɪꜱ ʙᴀᴄᴋ ᴀɢᴀɪɴꜱᴛ ᴛʜᴇ ᴄᴏʟᴅ bones. The air smelled like mildew and rot. He could hear Cole calling his name, but his brother's voice was muffled, distant, and fading fast.

Frigid air swept across Tinn's skin. The Thing was moving around him.

HELLO, CHANGELING. It was not a proper voice. It was like the echo of a voice.

"What do you want?" Tinn managed.

YOU, said the Thing. **I'VE BEEN WAITING.**

"Why me?" The Thing was moving behind him now, and Tinn turned to face it, not that he could see anything.

196

YOU KNOW.

"Is it because I'm—" Tinn swallowed. He looked down at his hands again and saw that they had lost their viny texture. They now looked as if they were made from the same smoky fabric as the Thing's cloak. "—because I'm a . . . a goblin?"

YOU ARE A WASTED GOBLIN. MAGIC WITHOUT PURPOSE. AND YOU ARE A FAILED HUMAN. YOU ARE NEITHER HERE NOR THERE.

"That's dumb. I'm here, obviously." Tinn tried to keep his voice steady and confident, but some part of him knew exactly what the Thing meant. He didn't belong. He had spent a lifetime not belonging, knowing that the terrible truth was coiled in wait deep down inside of him. He had spent a lifetime fearing it, hating himself for it, waiting for it to spring.

YES. YOU FEEL IT. YOU HAVE ALWAYS FELT IT. IT HAS SEASONED YOU. IT HAS MADE YOU READY FOR ME.

Tinn wiped his face. "Okay. So, what now? Are you going to eat me or something?"

YES.

"Oh." Tinn swallowed. That was not the response he had been hoping for. "You could . . . not eat me, instead."

I WILL FEED ON YOUR FEAR AND DEVOUR YOUR DESPAIR, the voice continued. **THERE ARE NOT ENOUGH WORDS IN YOUR WORLD FOR ALL OF THE PARTS OF YOU THAT I WILL CONSUME.**

"You're going to eat my feelings?"

AND SO MUCH MORE THAN THAT. I WILL PULL THE MISERY FROM YOUR BONES, CHANGELING, AND AS I DO, YOUR MISERY WILL BECOME YOU. AND THE MORE I DRAW FROM YOU, THE MORE EXQUISITE YOUR MISERY WILL GROW, UNTIL MISERY IS ALL THAT IS LEFT OF YOU. ONLY THEN WILL I FINISH YOU OFF AND ADD YOUR BONES TO MY NEST.

"Wow. Okay. So you're just a whole pile of evil. Um. Why are you telling me all that, though? If you're going to torture me, why haven't you just begun?"

YOU THINK THAT I HAVE NOT BEGUN? The Thing made a wheezing noise that might have been a laugh. It made Tinn's insides feel gross. **RUN, CHANGELING**, the Thing said at last.

The vines hanging over Tinn's head spread apart ever so slightly, and the path of ivory bones became just barely visible in the gloom.

Tinn hesitated. "You're—you're letting me go?"

I AM LETTING YOU HOPE, said the Thing. It laughed again, a horrible, dry laugh.

Tinn ran.

"It's okay," Annie repeated over and over, holding Cole tight. "It's okay. I've got you."

Cole shook his head. He wanted it to be true, but finally he pushed his head up and wiped his eyes with his hands. "No," he said. "It's not okay."

Annie brushed his hair out of his face. "Tell me everything."

So Cole told his mother about Candlebeard and the maze of thorns and about the terrible, horrible Thing lurking inside them. He told his mother about Tinn—about what he had done, what he had said, and what he had become within the bramble.

"Oh, it's na fair!" Kull wailed, throwing his head back when Cole was done.

"Suddenly you care about my children?" Annie arched an eyebrow at the goblin.

"I care about the one that's still lost! Yer manling here says his face was all shadows and vines. Aye, boy?"

Annie shook her head. "I'm sure it was the shadows from the—"

"Yer sure o' nothin'!" Kull spat. "I seen it before. Skin like smoke? Shiftin' ta look like his surroundin's? He *changed*."

Annie bit her lip.

"Otch! Three of the wee brats ta choose from, an' them brambles had to take *my* changelin'! Tonight of all nights.

199

Oh, I should've stolen him back ages ago. Ohhh . . ." Kull rubbed his face with his hands and trailed off into incoherent mumbles.

"What's special about tonight?" said Fable.

The miserable little goblin peered up through his fingers.

"Tonight's the night of the full moon," said Cole. "That's what the letter said, right? It said if the changeling wasn't back in the horde by the full moon, he would die. All the goblins would die."

Kull nodded.

"But why? Why are you going to die? What do the goblins want with my brother? What does everyone want with my brother?"

Kull groaned. "Goblin matters is fer goblin ears," he grumbled.

"Answer him, thief," said the queen. "Your secrets are worth nothing if you're not alive to keep them."

Kull sighed deeply. She was not wrong. "The changelin' has always been at the heart of it. It's how the whole trick works."

"Explain yourself," the queen demanded.

"S'about balance," said Kull, "between this world and t'other. Goblin magic isn'a like the magic on t'other side, see? We dinna bend reality into pretty shapes like them fancy fairy folk do, we just gives the universe a teensie nudge an' do the rest fer ourselves. Goblin power is chaos magic—the power o' luck. But we do need magic ta live. Like fish need water, all the oddlings on this side o' the barrier need at least a little magic. Canna survive without it. The thing is, fer magic ta exist in this world, the other side needs somethin' in return. Trade. Goblins is good at trades."

"Me," said Cole. "You were going to trade me to the other side for more magic. That's why you tried to take me when I was a baby, isn't it?"

Kull nodded. "The changelin' ritual is a sacred thing. When a changelin' is born, 'tis born with all the magic of the horde in one wee body, which makes the other side pull even harder ta get 'im. The trick is: iffin a human baby goes ta the other side, then the Earth will pull back against the veil for the earthly child, just the same way. That's the trick, see? A changelin' trades places with a human baby so that human baby can be given to the fairies on t'other side. Magic child here, earthly child there. Balance. Water out, water in—an' we fishies keep swimmin'."

"But that's awful!" Annie said.

Kull shrugged.

"Did you leave a changeling in *my* place?" asked the queen.

"I wasn'a on the council then," said Kull. "Before my time. But aye. Probably. The changelin' in yer stead would've long since come back ta the horde an' become kin an' kind again. That's what the old scrolls say. Na supposed ta stay. Changelin' magic isn'a meant ta last forever."

"I thought you didn't even want the children," Annie growled. "It was the fairies who wanted them. That's what you said."

"Aye. We dinna want the children. We want the *magic*. We need it. Just a little. Just enough. The children just . . . help us get it."

"Not anymore, they don't," said the queen. Her glare could have cut glass.

"Na," agreed Kull sorrowfully. "Na anymore. Na without that changelin'. We're done, we are. 'Tis the end o' the horde. Dinna look so smug about it. 'Tis the end o' magic in yer Wild Wood, too, witchy."

The queen scowled.

"Oh, did ya think yer fancy forest was special on its own? Na. That's us. We're na totally selfish, see? We share the magic we bring. At least, we did when there was magic ta share. All over now, of course. But ya already knew that, didn't ya?"

The queen scowled again, but did not respond.

"What's he talking about, Mama?" Fable said. "What's going to happen to our forest?"

"It will still be the same forest," said the queen.

"Ha!" Kull barked. "Same trees an' rocks, maybe. Na more fair folk, though. Na more oddlings. Na that there's a whole lot left, anymore. The smart ones is them that already left. Them that stay, they won't stay the same, na without magic. We'll all wither inta something less, we will. Something mortal. Na more hinky lights. Na more goblins. Na more wee girlies who can also be bears."

"Me?" Fable's eyes flashed to her mother. "Am *I* magic, Mama?"

The queen took a deep breath.

"Ya daft girlie." Kull shook his head. "Didja think ya were human?"

Fable's eyes bored into her mother.

The queen sighed. "Maybe you could be," she said, "once and for all—like I never had the chance to be. Things come to an end, child."

"Stop it," Annie said. Her jaw set and she drew a long, determined breath. "You're all talking as if my son is gone, but he's not! He's in there! He is right in front of us!" She jabbed a finger at the bramble. "Tinn is alive in there

203

somewhere, and he needs me, and I am not leaving this forest without him!"

The Queen of the Deep Dark regarded her thoughtfully. "I am with you, Annie Burton. My heart is with you. The whole forest is with you. But what would you have us do?"

"Otch. Blast it. I'm goin' in."

Both women turned their eyes to Kull. He did not have Annie's fury, but he wore his resigned determination like an itchy uniform.

"Bramble needs a body. Iffin I can find him, it can have mine. It'll pay a bit of my debt, at least. Clear some red ink outta my ledger after all these years. Iffin I *can't* find him, well . . ." He swallowed. "It's the same fer me in the end either way, innit?"

"Wait," said the queen.

Kull looked up at her. "Dinna try an' stop me."

"Of course not. You are the obvious and most expendable choice. Besides, goblin hide is tougher than human skin. You will make greater distance in less time, however, if I throw you into the center rather than let you wade in from the edge. Hold still."

Fifty feet away, a great commotion erupted out of the thickest part of the bramble. Fluttering shadows rose in drifts like ashes from the vines, and then a bubble of pure, smooth darkness began to coalesce. It swelled, inflating like a great ebony balloon, until it was as tall as a house. The darkness was so absolute, it was like a hole in the forest.

"Maybe," said Fable, "we should go check out that thing before we toss anybody into the middle of the stabby death vines?"

THIRTY-ONE

Tɪɴɴ's ᴀʀᴍs ʙᴜʀɴᴇᴅ ꜰʀᴏᴍ ᴀ ʜᴜɴᴅʀᴇᴅ ᴛɪɴʏ cuts as he half ran, half fell through the shrinking tunnel of thorns. Escape was his only thought. The Thing followed with deliberate slowness. It filled the thorny corridor behind him. When the corridor expanded, the Thing expanded. It was always just as close whenever Tinn dared to glance back, its body shrouded in tattered shadows, its face hidden in darkness.

Feelings swelled in Tinn's chest. There was fear, of course—his heart pounded with it. There was sadness—it welled up in his throat. Anger, desperation, panic—

And cold.

The unnatural cold washed over him and through him. His fingers were numb. His whole body ached. It was an empty ache of unfeeling, which was somehow worse than pain. Little by little, the numbness crept into his skull. Tinn tore through the vines ahead of him, no longer feeling the sting of their barbs or the pull of the cords at all. His vision blurred and his head ached. It was becoming harder to focus, harder to think. Bones crunched and crackled beneath his feet. Terrible words that had been hiding at the back of his mind grew louder and louder, until soon they were echoing in his mind like cannon fire.

I don't belong.

I will never belong.

I am alone.

The Thing was inside his head. The thoughts were his own, Tinn knew—he had kept them buried within himself for many years—but it was the Thing that was pulling them out of him. He glanced backward. It was right behind him.

With his lungs burning from effort and panic and the biting cold, Tinn made a final desperate leap and found himself bursting free of the nest of vines at last. The thorny brambles fell behind him, and Tinn tumbled to the open ground, panting. He was free. He was finally free.

So why was it still so dark? Had night fallen? Tinn pushed himself up. Above him hung a dome of perfect darkness, an empty, starless void. He wasn't looking at the sky at all, he realized with a heavy weight in his chest. He was in the center of a bubble of inky black. It didn't matter that he had escaped the vines—he was still completely trapped.

OF COURSE YOU ARE TRAPPED, the voice echoed in his mind. **YOU HAVE BEEN TRAPPED FROM THE MOMENT YOU SET FOOT IN THIS FOREST. THIS IS HOW IT WAS ALWAYS GOING TO END, CHANGELING. I AM YOUR PURPOSE. I AM YOUR ANSWER.**

Slowly, Tinn turned around.

The Thing was there, sliding out of the bramble, unhurried.

"Why are you doing this?" Tinn screamed. "Why let me run at all? Why are you just toying with me?"

I WAITED FOR YOU, the creature answered, calmly. **NOW I AM SAVORING YOU. HOPE IS SUCH A TANTALIZING TORMENT.**

The shadows danced and bobbed across the creature the way moonlight ripples across water. It was difficult to tell where the Thing ended and the dark dome began. There was light, light enough to see the earth at his feet and make out the edges of the creature, but where the light was coming from he could not guess. Before he could give the matter much thought, the words thundered in his skull again.

I am alone.

The force of the thought made Tinn's head hurt. His legs gave out and he sank to his knees.

I am alone. I am alone. I am alone.

YES, said the Thing. **YOU WERE ALWAYS ALONE.**

"Shut up," Tinn said, but his voice sounded small and far away.

THEY ARE DELICIOUS, THESE FEELINGS, said the creature. **AND SUCH POWER BEHIND THEM.** The Thing breathed in deeply. **I MISS THE MAGIC.**

"Maybe there would still be magic around if you didn't go eating everybody!" Tinn managed.

IT IS TRUE. THE FOREST IS DYING. I PLAYED MY PART IN THIS. The Thing's voice was dry and emotionless. **THE MAGIC OF THIS PLACE WILL END, AND I WILL END WITH IT. BUT SO BE IT. I WILL SAVOR EVERY MOMENT OF ITS PASSING.**

The air felt thin as Tinn tried to catch his breath.

YOU DO NOT BELONG HERE. NOR ANYWHERE. YOU HAVE NEVER HAD A PLACE IN THIS WORLD—NOT WITH THE GOBLINS WHO ABANDONED YOU.

The Thing moved closer. Tinn's legs felt weak.

NOT WITH THE HUMANS WHO DESPISE YOU.

It was circling him, but Tinn could not find the energy to follow the creature any longer. He let his head sag and let the Thing's voice wash against him like waves against a ship.

The creature sighed. In a twisted way, its sigh reminded Tinn of the way his mother sighed when she took fresh bread out of the oven and breathed in the sweet, warm smell of it—a contented sigh, a hungry sigh—and that happy memory stung his heart even more.

AH, YES, breathed the creature. **FAMILY. PRECIOUS FAMILY. YOU HAVE ONLY EVER BROUGHT SUFFERING TO THE PEOPLE YOU CALL FAMILY, AND THEY WERE NEVER REALLY YOURS, WERE THEY? YOU HAVE NEVER HAD A HOME. YOU HAVE NEVER HAD A REAL MOTHER.**

Tinn's lungs were slowly turning to ice.

YOU HAVE NEVER HAD A REAL BROTHER.

The world was tipping. Tinn felt sick. He couldn't tell if he was falling or floating or not moving at all. He shut his eyes tight.

SHE HAS ALREADY FOUND HIM, YOU KNOW, the creature taunted. Tinn could feel the wet breath of the Thing on his neck. **THEY WILL LEAVE THIS FOREST TOGETHER AND LEAVE YOU BEHIND. YOU ARE ALONE, CHANGELING.**

"She found him?" Tinn said. Inexplicably, the spinning world ground to a stop. Tinn opened his eyes.

The creature was inches away from his face now, but Tinn did not flinch. He took slow, deep breaths as he

210

surveyed the Thing. Up close, the shadows that made up its cloak looked more like smoke than solid fabric.

"My mother found Cole?" Tinn asked again. His voice didn't sound quite so far away anymore. "They're together? They're safe?"

The creature hesitated. **SHE DOES NOT WANT YOU. HE DOES NOT NEED YOU.**

Tinn took a slow, deep breath. Had the creature backed away a few paces?

YOU ARE LOST, it said, angrily. **YOU ARE ALONE!**

"Yeah," said Tinn. "I suppose I am." And in spite of himself, in spite of everything, Tinn smiled. "But it's nice to know that my mom and Cole are not."

Above them, the creature's shell of living shadows cracked.

Tinn squinted as white light poured through the fractures in the Thing's dark dome. He smelled pine needles and wet earth, and for just a moment he heard birdsong and felt a warm summer breeze on his face.

Behind Tinn, the Thing made a strangled, angry noise. The shadows that formed the obsidian dome slid and scrambled over themselves to seal the gap and keep out the blinding light, but it was too late. Tinn's eyes had already begun to adjust, and just beyond the bubble he had seen them. The queen was there in her furry cloak. On one side of her stood Fable and on the other a small man with floppy, pointed ears. And there, not twenty feet away from Tinn, were Cole and his mother, hand in hand. Tinn's heart pounded against his ribs.

The light dimmed and the image vanished as the shadows flung themselves desperately over the gaps. They were thin, wispy things, and light still crept through them. The sunbeams grew dim and choked, but they were unyielding. From within, the globe no longer looked pure, inky black. It was gray, etched with myriad splintery cracks, like glistening spiderwebs.

THEY CANNOT REACH YOU HERE, the Thing intoned, but its voice had lost its cold confidence. The cracks in the bubble were widening, and the shadows holding it together along the seams were stretched nearly transparent in their effort to keep the dome intact. **YOU ARE ALONE.**

Tinn turned back to the Thing. Was it smaller? He watched with fascination as shadows peeled off the Thing's cloak to feed the faltering dome. For just an instant, as the inky layers shifted, he saw something deep inside the cloak of shadows shudder.

"Of course I'm not alone," said Tinn.

YOU ARE LIKE ME. YOU DO NOT BELONG. YOU ARE ALONE. YOU ARE ALONE. YOU ARE ALONE.

"Like you?" Tinn said. "Wait. Are *you* lonely?"

Tinn's fear began to slip away.

At that moment the Thing—tired and hungry and, yes, profoundly lonely—decided to just eat the brat quickly and get the whole thing over with.

Tinn's vision went black.

THIRTY-TWO

ANNIE HELD TIGHT TO COLE'S HAND AS THEY all approached the enormous orb together. Kull reached out a finger and touched it. "Otch! Hard as iron, that is, an' cold as ice."

"It is a complete dome," the queen announced, walking the perimeter. "No holes or windows, except perhaps where it overlaps the vines."

Fable had already become a cub and was burrowing at the base of the dome where it touched down on the forest floor.

"Fable, be careful," her mother chided. "Don't get so close."

"Goes way down," Fable announced when she was a girl again. "I couldn't feel a bottom. It's really cold. I don't like it."

"Do you hear that?" said Cole. "Everybody stop talking! Listen!"

The group fell silent. For several seconds the only sounds in the forest were distant birdcalls and the steady shuffle of the wind blowing through branches. Annie squeezed Cole's hand. And then the dome before them shuddered, the cracks sealing themselves as quickly as they had appeared.

"He's there!" Annie shouted. "He's inside!"

"You're sure?" The queen had seen something within the globe. It might have been a boy, but it had been as shadowy as the dome itself.

Annie threw herself at the dome, pounding and scratching, but she might as well have been attacking a glacier. Her hands tingled from the impact of each blow and the icy cold of the obsidian wall. In another moment, the great grizzly was beside her. She felt heat radiating off the queen's flank as the bear reared up and raked the dome with her massive paws. Not a mark remained.

"Argh! It's no good," Annie cried. "It won't budge." She kicked the wall, and the impact only sent a shudder of pain up her leg.

"No, look!" called Cole. "Something's happening! You're doing it!"

Annie took a step back. "I don't think we did that." Above them, the inky surface was swirling and rippling angrily. "Back away, kids."

Before any of them could move, the entire dome burst like an enormous bubble. Shreds of shadow fell to earth like freshly shed snakeskins. Where the ghostly coils touched the ground, the grass turned to ash. Within the perimeter of dead earth stood two figures, each covered in a matching fabric of darkness.

"Tinn!" Annie cried.

Tinn did not turn toward the sound of his mother's voice. The shadows that had hung above his head were now dangling off him, clinging like a tattered, wet sheet. The Thing had traded Tinn's high-domed prison for a suffocating funeral shroud. Tinn struggled, his hands reaching and grasping blindly, but the blanket of blackness completely enclosed him.

"Let him go!" Annie shouted.

IT IS TOO LATE.

"Like heck it is!" Fable launched herself forward.

The Thing made the faintest motion with one hand and the fallen strips of shadow littering the earth took on a new life, swelling and coiling as they became living vines once more. The nearest cord snatched Fable off the ground midstep and hung her, kicking and struggling, in the chilly air.

The bear-queen was at her daughter's side in an instant, snarling as her talons tore at the reborn briars.

THE GIRL WILL BE THE NEXT TO DIE, a voice echoed across the forest.

The bear bellowed with rage.

Annie had already jumped into the mess, ducking and dodging the slithering vines as she tried to make her way closer to Tinn.

Cole pulled the penknife from his pocket and darted after her, but the thorns caught him by the feet and pitched him forward onto his hands and knees. The knife bounced away across the charred earth. "Mom!"

Annie froze, turning back to Cole. In her moment of distraction, the vines caught her around her waist, pinning her halfway between her sons.

The voice laughed darkly. **YOU HAVE ALREADY LOST.**

Kull bit his lip, shifting from one foot to the other at the edge of the circle. The children were all caught. The woman had buried herself in the nest of thorns, and even the bear, for all its terrible strength, was scarcely able to keep itself free of the vines, let alone rescue anyone. What good could Kull possibly do?

In the corner of his vision, a tiny, flickering light appeared. He paid it no attention until it was joined by another, and another. Finally, Kull tore his eyes from the vines and looked up. Emerging from the trees came one bald head and then a second, two bushy beards, and a third. A dozen glowing candles. Twenty. Fifty.

"The hinkypunks," gasped Cole, as they began swarming through the trees to surround the circle of dead earth and slithering shadows. Where their candlelight touched the darkness, the vines shrank back.

Dangling sideways from the vines, Fable shook the hair out of her eyes. "Hey! The hinkypunks came back!"

Cole stood up. For just a moment, he ceased kicking at the cords around his ankles and watched the figures filing in.

"Na just the hinkies," Kull whispered.

Behind the crowd of hinkypunks came flittering wings and the sound of heavy footsteps that shook the earth.

A familiar face emerged from the throng. Candlebeard nodded solemnly as he stepped up to Cole. Silently, the hinkypunk plucked the candle from his chest and held its flame to the dark vines at the boy's feet. The cords shuddered at the sudden heat, and the moment they slackened, Cole jumped free from their grip.

"No more," Candlebeard said. "I let it take so many of them. I will not let it take another. Not one more hinkypunk, nor human, nor goblin, nor bird, nor beast. No more."

On every side, the forest was abuzz with sound. Cole could see creatures of all shapes and sizes emerging from the shadows: feathers and fur, horns and halos. He blinked up at a tremendous eagle, a snow-white stag so pure it seemed to glow, and a muscular man with the lower body of a stallion. They had all come back to reclaim the Wild Wood. The forest itself seemed to shiver at their return.

Kull watched with a lump in his throat as one last faction crested the ridge. Chief Nudd and the rest of the goblin horde clambered over the rise like a tidal wave, every one of them dressed for war. He could see his kinfolk, Brynn and Gubb, swinging the dwarven axes he had traded them in exchange for rare scrolls. Runty little Pall was wearing her prized boar-skull helmet. Kull smiled. He had helped Pall fell that pig decades ago. That was when she had still been speaking to Kull, long before he had doomed them all with his stupid mistake. Chief Nudd pushed through the crowd, and for a tense moment Kull braced himself for the usual crippling reprimand.

Nudd put a hand on Kull's shoulder. He spoke only four words: "We're with ya, idjit."

The knot in Kull's throat tightened, and bubbling up in his chest he felt a warmth he had almost forgotten he could feel. He nodded, his eyes watering. *We.* It had been a long time since Kull had been part of a *we.* Without speaking, he turned toward the thorny chaos ahead of him. At the center of it all, his changeling needed him.

Annie pulled in vain against the vines. Cole was free. That strange bearded man had released him. For the moment, her only concern became reaching Tinn. Making sense of a world in which the myriad figures emerging from the trees were real would have to wait until after her son was safe.

Tinn was still there in the center of the circle, still struggling against the shroud of darkness, but his movements had become slow and weak. Over his shoulder stood a horrible, hooded figure. Its cloak melted into the vines stretching out all around them and into the shadows that were choking her son. Annie shivered.

Vines as tough as iron chains had wrapped themselves

around her wrists, her waist, her legs, and the harder she tugged, the tighter they clung.

To Annie's left, a half dozen little men with big bushy beards were busy with Fable's rescue. The great bear was beneath the girl when the vines gave way under the heat of the candle flames, so that Fable landed safely on her mother's back when she fell. To Annie's right, a flurry of motion erupted as Kull and a dozen goblins came bursting through the briars.

"Clear 'em off!" Kull commanded, and at once the goblins were all around her.

A particularly tiny goblin wearing a pig's skull for a hat grabbed the vine at Annie's wrist. The scrappy creature tugged and gnawed on the pernicious coil until it finally released Annie and snapped around the goblin instead.

"Success!" the goblin squeaked gleefully as the vine slowly pulled her to the ground.

A fat goblin in a chain mail vest grabbed hold of the thick vine around Annie's waist and soon found himself taking Annie's place as its victim. One by one, the goblins coaxed her bindings off her and onto themselves until Kull was pulling with all his strength at the last cord binding her ankles, but the vine refused to yield.

"Kull, stop! Don't worry about me, save Tinn!"

"I am, ya daft womern," he barked. The cord finally

jerked loose and he fell over backward into the mess. "Go!" he hollered.

Free at last, Annie raced toward Tinn. All around rang the yells, whoops, and snarls of countless strange creatures banding together to fight the bramble, but as she reached the center of the circle, all sounds ceased. A cushion of absolute silence met her as she knelt before her son.

YOU HAVE COME TO WATCH HIM DIE, the Thing's voice boomed. The creature hovering just behind Tinn was the shape of a man, near enough, but it did not move like a man. It sagged and swayed, like an under-stuffed scarecrow.

Annie ignored the wretched creature and reached a hand out to Tinn's face to pull the shadows off him. The shroud was not a single sheet, but a patchwork of ragged slices of darkness that melted together like thick molasses. They were so cold they burned Annie's skin. Solid and smoky and liquid all at once, they slid through her grasp, clinging to her fingers and closing back over the boy's face as quickly as she could pull them away.

HE IS NOT YOURS. NOT ANYMORE.

Annie abandoned her efforts to pull the darkness away and threw her arms around Tinn's neck instead. It was like holding packed snow in the shape of a boy, but she did not let go. Tears welled in her eyes. She thought about winter nights, about tiptoeing into her boys' room to pull the covers up to their chins so that they would be safe and warm in their beds.

Tinn had stopped moving.

YOU HAVE ALREADY LOST HIM.

Annie held her son tight. Hot tears rolled off her cheeks. Where they touched the shroud of darkness, the shadows began to melt away.

STOP, the Thing commanded.

Annie felt a tremble beneath her fingers, no stronger at first than a fluttering moth's wings, but growing. She looked down to see a head emerging from the shadows. Beneath the shroud, Tinn's face was gray-green. As she watched, wicked thorns grew from his skin. She winced as the barbs pierced her arms. But she did not let go.

Tinn lifted his chin, his eyes unfocused and full of confusion. "Mom?" he breathed at last.

And then he saw his own reflection in his mother's eyes. "I don't know how to control it," he whispered plaintively.

Annie nodded and held him tighter. "It's okay, Tinn." He could have been made of fire and she would not have let him go. "I've got you."

"I'm not—" His voice caught in his throat, each word crumbling like brittle straws. "I'm not your real boy. It's Cole. It's always been Cole."

"Of course you're my real boy." Annie squeezed tighter

still, closing her eyes against the pain of the stabbing thorns and the burning cold. "And you will always be my boy."

Slowly, the cold ebbed, the barbs dulled, and Annie felt shaking hands hugging her back. She rocked Tinn in her arms until he finally stopped shivering, and when she bent to kiss his forehead, it was the dirty pink forehead she had kissed countless times in the past thirteen years.

Footsteps pounded behind them, and they both looked up in time to see Cole pelting across the charred ground. He nearly knocked them over as he joined the embrace, tears and laughter mixing as they pressed together. In that brief giddy moment, that hug in the eye of the storm, the cold fell away completely.

"See, huggin' is na the sorta thin' I'm good at," Kull said from behind them. "Wouldn'a even have thought o' it. Just na a hugger." He limped up to them, free of the vines, but not without a few fresh scars. He gave Tinn a wink as the boy looked up at him. "Hello, lad. Nice ta finally meet ya properly."

NO! The Thing's voice boomed across the forest, and the cushion of silence around them was gone. All around them, the commotion of creatures battling the bramble returned. **I WILL END YOU ALL!**

"That's enough!" cried a raspy, gravelly voice.

Candlebeard stood atop a pile of vines right behind the Thing. "It's over."

YOU ARE A FOOL. WHAT DO YOU THINK IS GOING TO HAPPEN? DO YOU REALLY THINK THAT THESE ARE YOUR ALLIES? YOU THINK YOU ARE FRIENDS? THE GOBLIN WOULD SELL YOU OUT IN AN INSTANT TO SAVE HIS HORDE. THE WITCH WOULD BURY EVERY LAST ONE OF YOU TO PROTECT HER CHILD. THE WOMAN WOULD LET THIS WHOLE FOREST BURN TO ASHES IF IT WOULD SAVE HER FAMILY. YOU MISERABLE, BROKEN OLD MAN. DO YOU THINK THERE WILL BE A PLACE FOR YOU WHEN THIS IS OVER? AFTER EVERYTHING YOU'VE DONE?

The vines at Candlebeard's feet began to climb up his legs. He did not struggle against them. He only watched as they slowly circled his body. From behind their barbs, his little candle quivered.

"I did everything wrong," Candlebeard said. "But it's never too late to do something right."

Lights twinkled around the perimeter of the ashen circle as the other hinkypunks silently observed the proceedings.

"He would be proud of you," Cole called across the vines. "He would be so proud."

The flame in Candlebeard's chest swelled. "Your father would be proud of you, too," he replied. "You're a boy worth coming back for."

The light expanded until Cole found he could not look at Candlebeard directly, and in an instant the vines were aflame. From every side, dancing fires pulsed in concert with Candlebeard's, and soon the bramble was burning all around them.

The heat stung Tinn's cheeks, but even as the flames danced above their heads, a curious calm came over him. Fear and anger melted away, and in their absence he regarded the Thing with new eyes. The wretched creature looked very small now. It pulled the shadows closer, like a child tugging the blankets up to its chin.

"I saw you," said Tinn, softly. "I saw what you are underneath. It's okay. You don't have to be afraid anymore."

NO, spat the Thing. **YOU DO NOT KNOW WHAT I AM!** Its cloak of shadows was falling to pieces, molting and shrinking before Tinn's eyes. The Thing, which had once loomed over Tinn, was no larger than a stray dog now, and getting smaller. It frantically pulled more shadows toward itself, and as it did so, the few unburnt vines around the clearing sagged and crumpled. **YOU ARE THE ONE WHO IS AFRAID!** it boomed.

"I was." Tinn nodded. "I was afraid of all sorts of things—the woods and the witch and wild animals, and I was afraid of you. But I'm not afraid now. You don't have to be afraid, either."

WHAT ARE YOU DOING? The echoes had left the Thing's voice, and it sounded much smaller now. Indeed, it looked like little more than a sooty house cat in a pile of old black socks. Still the shadows dropped away from it, melting like slivers of ice in the flickering firelight.

"You're not in that place anymore," Tinn told it. "You're free."

STOP TALKING. NO. NO. NO. The last of the shadows finally fell away, and the Thing stood before them, naked and shivering. It was no larger than a mouse, its snout pointed like a shrew's, its ears drooping and tattered.

The fire was already beginning to die down, as quickly as it had started. The only motion from the vines was the occasional pop of a spark and the settling of the charred remains. The bramble was dead. In the drifting ashes, the tiny, defeated Thing quivered.

Tinn leaned down and tenderly scooped up the trembling creature. He could feel its tiny heart racing.

"I didn't want to believe that we were the same," he whispered to the Thing. "But you were right. I come from an in-between place, too. Only, nobody ever came for you, did they? That isn't fair." The Thing wriggled to free itself, but Tinn cupped his hands together to contain it. "You did terrible things. It's not up to me to forgive the things you did. But I am sorry that you suffered. You didn't deserve that. You didn't deserve to be turned into this."

The trembling Thing turned its eyes to Tinn, twin

beads of glistening black. And then, ever so gingerly, it opened its mouth and chomped down hard on the round part of Tinn's palm.

"Ow!" Tinn dropped the Thing, and it raced away amid the vines.

"Otch! Get back here, ya wee demon!" Kull scampered after the creature, swatting and stomping at it fruitlessly as it flitted away under the ash and embers.

Tinn rubbed the place where the Thing had bitten him. It felt sore and strangely hot. The weight of the day's adventures felt like it was pressing down on him all at once, making his head swim.

"Are you okay?" Cole was saying, but his voice sounded far away.

Tinn looked at his palm. The skin was soft—as soft as the fabric on his mother's dress. It rippled and became a drab green again, and then rich brown hair sprouted along his arm. He could do nothing to control the changes. Tinn was finding it harder and harder to breathe.

His knees wobbled, and a moment later he felt his mother's arms holding him again. He leaned into her. Even in the middle of the Deep Dark Forest, his mother smelled like baking flour and honey and . . . and home. He smiled blearily. He wanted to speak, but the words got lost before they ever found his mouth.

"What's happening to him?" Annie said.

"My changelin'," Kull said, reverently, "is comin' back." Tinn managed to turn his head to face the goblin. The whole forest was spinning. "When all this is done, ya'll look like ya was always supposed to, lad," the goblin told him. "Kin an' kind. Ya'll finally be one o' us again. Ya'll be the best of us." He gave Tinn a toothy smile that he probably hoped was reassuring.

Tinn felt something, but he was not reassured. His tongue ran along the sharp teeth in his mouth, and his stomach twisted. He turned his glistening eyes back to his mother's face. She was fading in and out of focus. Tinn was losing her. He wanted to speak, he wanted to call out before she faded away forever, but his throat was too tight and his mind too muddled.

His mother spoke one word, just before the world faded away. It was only one word, but it was a word Tinn needed to hear. His muscles relaxed, and his mother held him, limp in her arms. "Always," she repeated. "Always. Always. Always."

THIRTY-THREE

THE VOYAGE TO THE HOLLOWCLIFF HORDE came to Tinn in waves and flashes as he drifted in and out of consciousness. There were trees and hills and big rocks, and soon they were winding down a narrow path along the face of a steep cliff. It was just the sort of thing Cole would have loved, Tinn mused, sleepily. Where was Cole? Were humans allowed into the horde?

When Tinn opened his eyes again, he found himself gazing up at a rocky ceiling in a dimly lit cave. The air smelled like seawater and something sweet—chocolate? He sat up. He was resting on a small bed. His hands had been treated and wrapped with soft linen. The skin beneath them was a pale, greenish gray, but it had stopped changing. Were his fingers shorter? In his mouth he could still feel sharp fangs. Was this who he was now? A few feet away, a goblin wearing a weathered felt top hat with a spray of bright red cardinal feathers tucked in the brim was pouring something from a steaming copper pot into little clay cups.

"Ah. Yer timin' is perfect, lad," the goblin said softly.

"Oh. Um. Who are you?"

"Name is Nudd, son of Gwynn, high chief o' the Hollowcliff Horde, and maker"—he gave Tinn a wink—"of a grand hot cocoa."

"You . . . you made me cocoa?"

"Aye." The goblin handed Tinn a cup. "Drink up, lad. Yer brother's had three already, and some cakes. Dinna worry. I have a few put aside fer you."

Tinn took the cup, still staring at Nudd. "My brother? Is he here? Is my mom?"

"Aye, and the witches and a hinky. I had ta boot half the forest out of the cave when ya first arrived. Yer ma and brother took the longest ta convince. They're just outside now."

"Can I see them?"

"Soon enough. I think we need a wee chat first, just you and me."

Tinn took a deep breath. He nodded. "If you don't mind, Mr. Nudd, please—could you first tell me . . ." Tinn hesitated. "What do I look like?"

"Right handsome," Nudd assured him.

"Handsome like a person, or handsome like . . ."

Chief Nudd pulled a stool over to the bedside and sat down. "Do ya know what ya are, lad?"

"I'm a goblin, aren't I? A . . . a changeling?"

"That's right. Do ya know what that means?"

"I . . . change?"

The chief took a deep breath. "Okay. Right. Basics first."

Fable sat with her feet dangling off the goblin landing. Down below her, waves washed against the feet of the cliffs, and up above the last of the color was fading from the sky.

"Fable?" The boards creaked and swayed ever so slightly as her mother came to stand beside her. "Are you all right?"

"Mama, am I human?"

"Of course you are. You are my daughter."

"But I'm something else, too, aren't I?"

The queen pursed her lips. "Is this because of what that pesky thief, Kull, said about—"

"How does having a father work?" Fable turned to look at her mother at last. "Do I have a father?"

"This is neither the time nor the place for a delicate—"

"Tinn and Cole had a father. He went away, but at least they had one. Did my father go away, too? Is he human?"

"Fable . . ."

"Is he something else?"

"Fable, please."

"I want to know what I am!"

The queen leaned on the weathered railing and turned her eyes to the stars. She breathed with the rhythm of the waves for several seconds. "You had a father," she said, at last. "And, yes, he went away before you were born. But he doesn't define who you are."

"Are you mad at him?" Fable fidgeted with the railing. "For going away?"

"Furious," agreed the queen, but her voice did not sound angry. It sounded sad.

"Was he a bad man?"

The queen tore her eyes away from the stars and lowered herself to sit beside her daughter on the creaky platform. She wrapped one corner of the warm bearskin cloak around Fable's shoulders and Fable leaned into her mother. "Do you remember when I used to tell you bedtime stories," the queen said, "about the other side?"

"So that's what ya are," Chief Nudd finished, "the most sacred of our kind—a living bein' of luck and chaos incarnate."

Tinn swallowed. He did not feel like chaos incarnate. He felt exhausted. "So it's my fault," he managed. "I'm the reason magic is draining away from this side of the barrier. That other place, the Annwyn, is pulling magic away because of what I am. A changeling."

Nudd shook his head and clucked. "Nay, lad. The drain started before ya were born."

"But my being born made it worse."

Nudd took off his battered top hat and set it on the table. "Perhaps," he admitted. "But like everyone says: what makes things worse today will only make things better tomorrow."

"I'm pretty sure that's not something people say," said Tinn.

"Hm. Maybe it's just goblins. Anyway, our ancestors thought they had it figured out. The changelin' ritual solved everything. An earthly child stolen away, a magic child left behind. Balance ta both sides. Win-win."

"Except for the babies," said Tinn. "The ones you kidnapped to make it work."

"Right." Nudd winced. "I want ya ta understand, my father taught me that na child on Earth was e'er so beloved as a child in the Annwyn. I believed him, too. The fair folk raise human children as their own—lavish them with gifts, fill their every wakin' hour with joy an' wonder. Life is short an' miserable here on Earth, but children in the Annwyn can live two, maybe three hundred years. What sort of mother wouldn'a want her child ta live a long and glorious life in the Annwyn?"

"A mother who wanted to be a mother," said Tinn.

Nudd nodded soberly. "Yer a sharp lad, Tinn."

"Were they kind to you on the other side?" said Fable.

"More than kind." The queen held her daughter's arm. "I was their princess. I ate meals that tasted like sunbeams and wore dresses that shone like starlight. When I got older, they even taught me spells and charms. They smiled and laughed and applauded as I learned how to weave my own clumsy magic. One fairy gentleman smiled more kindly than the rest. He was young by fairy standards and fair by any."

"He was *fair*?"

"That means he was handsome. He made no advances, but over time I started to wish that he would. Years passed. He waited for me. Some of the fairy folk who had once applauded my lessons lost interest in me, but he did not.

He did not age. I did. When I was ready, I made my own advances. My fair gentleman did not protest."

"Did you kiss him?"

"There was a courtship, and there was a wedding, and there was a wedding night, and then one day I found I had conceived a child of my own."

"But did you *kiss* him?"

"Many times."

Fable smiled up at her mother, and then crinkled her brow. Her mother's eyes were glistening in the starlight. "Are these happy memories or sad ones?"

"Both," said the queen. "They were happy and sad times."

"Why were they sad?"

"For all the love I had for that place, those people, it was never my home. They were not unkind, but they were not my family. They had a name for me, but it was not my name. It all felt wrong, like a waking dream. I had been stolen. I did not want to be a mother in that place. I did not want my child to be born never knowing her real home. I did not want that for you, Fable. That place was not what my mother had wanted for me."

Fable looked down at the waves. "Can you still remember her?"

"I remember the sound of my mother's voice when she said my name." The queen's eyes drifted beyond the

236

dimming sunset. "And I remember a good-night kiss." She bent down and kissed Fable on the forehead. "I wish that I had more of her to remember."

Fable held her mother's hand beneath the cloak. "What did your *fair gentleman* think about you coming back to Earth?"

"I think it made him sad, but he promised me that he would take me back across the veil. Our child would know the Earth. He promised."

"Did he keep his promise?"

The queen took a deep breath and then gave Fable a smile that almost reached her eyes. "We're here, aren't we? And do you not know the Earth, child?"

Fable nodded, satisfied. "Did you ever get to see your mother again?"

The queen's gaze darkened as she stared out into the sea. The reflections of angry waves rolled across her eyes. She did not answer.

Fable tried another question: "Do you ever miss the other side?"

"No."

"Not even a little bit? Not even the part about being their princess?"

Her mother's jaw tightened. "I am no one's princess," said the queen.

"It was the old woman who changed my mind," Chief Nudd said. He poured Tinn another mug of chocolate. It was the last of the pot, thick and warm, and it made Tinn's whole chest feel hot as he sipped it. "My father was still chief when I met her. The old queen. The first queen. Yer witchy friend outside would be her spittin' image if she had a few more gray hairs and wrinkles. Anyway, she used ta have a wee little cabin in these woods, right on t'other side of the mire."

"I think I've seen it," said Tinn.

"She was a sad, sweet old thing," said Nudd. "Tried ta kill me several times. She had spirit, that one." He chuckled at the memory. "In the end we came ta understand each other. She gave me something I didn'a even know I needed, and in return I gave her a promise."

"What did she give you?"

"Forgiveness," he said, "for what my kind had done."

Tinn nodded. "What did you promise her in return?"

"I promised her that when I was chief," he said, "I would ne'er let another mother weep over an empty crib on our behalf. I meant it, too. So, when ya was born, with magic leavin' the Wild Wood an' the horde gettin' nervous, I found myself with quite the dilemma."

"You had to either risk your whole horde and keep your promise, or save your horde by stealing a child," said Tinn.

Nudd nodded. "Two bad options, neither fit fer the chief I'd swore I'd be. I thought I had a year ta make my choice. That's tradition. A changeling is always reared fer one year before the exchange, prepared ta take on its sacred role, taught how ta wield its powers, bonded ta the horde so it can find its way home. There are all manner o' rituals and ceremonies in that year."

"I don't remember any of them." Tinn shook his head.

Nudd winced. "That's because none of them ever happened. Ya met Kull, yes?"

Tinn nodded. "In the forest."

"Well, Kull's the one who muddled up the whole affair to begin with—but that's chaos magic fer ya. Iffin he hadn'a nudged the universe by stealin' ya, I might ne'er have found the third option."

"Third option?"

Nudd cackled. "When the veil between worlds is thin, magic can filter through. Just a little. Just enough. Every thirteen years, the barrier pulses and the veil gets a wee bit thinner. Goblins call this time the Veil Moon. At the height of the Veil Moon, a powerful goblin can slide into the fabric of the veil itself, inta the thin place in between, and give it a *nudge*. Iffin we nudge it just right, the universe gives us what we need."

"So, why don't you just do that? Why do you need me?"

"Generation by generation, the ceremony has become less effective. I performed it myself thirteen years ago, the year that you were born."

"What happened?"

"I just told you. *You were born.*" Nudd gave Tinn a wink. "The universe didn't give us any magic, but it gave us a changeling—the most powerful o' our kind in a generation, but also the most human o' our kind in history. More than a goblin. More than a man. Ya belong ta both worlds, boy. Yer neither here nor there. A goblin can push, a human can pull, but maybe—just maybe—a child o' both worlds can do both. If ya can do this, it'd mean we could all survive, lad. It'd mean na more children stolen from their cribs. Magic could live in the Wild Wood again."

Tinn swallowed. It was precisely what the Thing had said to him within the shell of shadows. "You need me because I'm neither here nor there," he whispered.

Nudd seemed to read his thoughts. "Yer no less goblin for being one of them," he said. "An' yer no less one of them fer being a goblin." He put a hand on Tinn's shoulder. "We need ya, lad. They need ya. The whole Wild Wood needs ya . . . ta be both."

THIRTY-FOUR

NIGHT HAD FALLEN THICK BY THE TIME TINN stepped out onto a creaking platform. He could hear waves breaking against the cliff below, and above him the stars twinkled in a blue-black sky. The goblin balcony jutted out over the ocean, suspended from the cliff by rusty chains. The landing was only as wide as the bed of a hay cart, and on either side, familiar faces lined the platform. Candlebeard and Kull stood to one side, Fable and the Queen of the Deep Dark to the other. At the end, his mother and brother waited.

All eyes turned toward Tinn as he emerged, and he was suddenly aware that he had no idea what face they were looking at. He still had not seen his goblin face—his real face. His whole life, he had only ever seen a reflection of his brother staring back at him from the mirror. His whole life, he had only ever *been* a reflection of his brother. Tinn's stomach turned. He had no idea who he really was. The stars blurred as the salty air stung his eyes. He blinked, trying not to cry. His legs felt weak, and Chief Nudd reached for an arm to steady him. Was the platform swaying? Tinn looked down. He felt like he might be sick. When he pulled his eyes up again, his mother was kneeling in front of him. She brushed her hand along his cheek.

"I guess this is me now," said Tinn, weakly. "I'm a goblin."

Annie wiped the tears from his face and pulled him close. "Oh, Tinn. You were always my little goblins, right from the start. My little goblin boys—both of you—and there's nothing in this world or the next that could ever change that."

"It's time," said Chief Nudd. Annie squeezed him close one last time, and then gradually stood and allowed the goblin chief to lead Tinn to the end of the platform.

Tinn glanced over his shoulder as they walked. The cliffs towering behind them were speckled with caves and tunnels. Copper pipes and wooden awnings had been bolted to the sheer rock face—and from every nook and cranny, atop every creaking, groaning structure, hung goblins. Anxious faces of gray and green and pallid yellow peered down at the platform, hanging from rusty scaffolding and leaning out skinny windows. None of them spoke a word as he crossed the wobbly boards. Tinn swallowed. The only sounds were the splash of the waves and the thud of his heart.

"Stand here, lad," Nudd said. "Ya'll only have a few moments. When the time is right, step through."

"Wait. How will I know when the time is right? What do I do when it is right? Are there words? A spell or something? I . . . I don't know how to do what you want me to do."

Nudd winked. "The universe knows how. You just give it a nudge."

"What does that—"

And then the air in front of Tinn crackled with electricity, and he could see it, a glimmer of an opening hanging in midair, right in front of him. Tinn could feel a tug, as if an invisible string was tied to his ribs, pulling him forward. He took a tentative step and then another. The hair on the backs of his arms stood on end. The sound of the waves swelled to a roar in his ears—and then everything went abruptly silent.

Tinn turned. His family was gone. The goblins were gone. The cliffs, the sea, the whole world was gone. There were no stars, Tinn realized, nor any light of any sort—but neither was there darkness.

Tinn tried to close his eyes and breathe deeply, but there was no air to fill his lungs, nor, he realized with horror, did he seem to have eyelids to close or lungs to fill. He could not feel sharp teeth in his mouth anymore, nor could he feel lips or a tongue. He could feel nothing but the persistent, gentle tug, like a current drawing him in.

Tinn concentrated, forcing himself to focus on Nudd's one instruction. With arms that weren't there, he reached out into the void. The fabric of the universe billowed and swayed around him. And Tinn gave it a nudge.

Cole's eyes were fixed on the place where his brother had vanished. One moment Tinn had been there, and then the next he was gone. Cole stared at the empty air until his eyes hurt. He could see it, rippling ever so faintly, the place where Tinn had crossed over.

The queen and the girl and the hinkypunk and the countless goblins all watched, too, and their collective silence made Cole's ears ache. It was as if the whole world was holding its breath.

And then, slowly, the platform grew brighter—not lighter, exactly, but more colorful, more vibrant. Cole shook his head to be sure he wasn't imagining the change. The dull, faded wood became a rich, mahogany brown. The rocks themselves shifted from slate gray to marbled blue. All around, the faces of countless goblins flushed from pale drabs to emerald greens. Their eyes shone like jewels as they smiled their toothy grins and laughed cackling laughs. With the color came a tingling warmth. It was the warmth of happy stories by the fire, a contented cat's purr, and fresh marmalade tarts. It was the summer sun on the branches of an old, knotted climbing tree. Cole stared until his eyes were watering.

The goblin chief held out his arms and closed his eyes, soaking up the sensation. The cardinal feathers in his hat were so brilliant, they might have been a little fire. Candlebeard's flame swelled. Up and down the cliff face and through the tunnels and caves erupted a joyful murmuring. The goblins cheered and laughed and danced. It was working. Whatever Tinn was doing, it was working.

Gradually the shimmering spot where Tinn had vanished began to shrink.

"Is it . . . closing?" Cole said.

Chief Nudd opened his eyes. His smile faltered.

"It's closing!" Cole yelled. "The gap is closing! Get him back!"

Nudd's shoulders fell. He looked at Cole miserably and shook his head.

"What are you waiting for?" Cole screamed, and then launched himself toward the shrinking spot at the end of the platform. "He's still in there! Tinn! TINN!"

THIRTY-FIVE

The first thing Tinn felt was heat. It was not unpleasant, a bit like reaching a hand into a hot bathtub, the warmth swirling around his fingers. The second thing Tinn felt was that he had fingers. He looked down. Everything was indistinct and blurry, as though he were engulfed in a heavy fog, but he had a body again! A goblin body, sure, but it was his.

Somewhere, just beyond his reach, he began to hear the rhythmic lapping of the ocean once more, and then a voice—his brother's. He drifted forward. They were there, just ahead, he could feel them, but he couldn't move any closer. The invisible string that had drawn him so gently inward had now gone taut. He pulled against it, straining to get back to his family, but the magical tether held him.

He glanced over his shoulder. Where there should have been nothing but open ocean, indistinct silhouettes loomed. Gradually they took the shape of valleys and hills. On the hills, strange creatures lumbered, bounded, flew across the alien terrain. With dawning clarity, Tinn realized he was looking into the Annwyn.

For a brief moment, Tinn felt himself drifting toward the fantastical landscape, but then came the jolt again, this time in the opposite direction. The invisible string holding him back from his world did not seem to want him to get too close to the world of magic, either.

"Tinn! TINN!"

The voice was muffled, but he could hear Cole calling him. He watched as if through frosted glass as his brother rushed forward toward him.

"I'm here! Cole, I'm here!" Tinn reached out his hand, stretching toward his brother—but Cole was thrown roughly backward, out of view. Tinn redoubled his efforts, frantically pulling against his bonds, but the harder he tried, the farther away the Earth seemed to drift. And then a grim thought occurred to him.

This was where *it* had lived. This was where the Thing

had been born, trapped for an eternity in the thin place between places, a prisoner without a home in either world. His breath came in anxious, shallow gulps.

The landscape before him began to fade, as if ice were spreading over the windowpane. The cliffs vanished into mist, then the queen, Kull, and finally Tinn's mother slipped away.

"No!" Tinn cried.

Cole was thrown backward, his fingers numb where they had touched the shimmering gap. Chief Nudd caught him before he could tumble clear off the platform and down into the choppy waters below. Cole felt like he had been run over by a bull.

"What happened?"

"Ya canna go after him," Nudd said soberly. "That's the fabric o' the universe itself."

"Well, the universe just took my brother! Get him back!"

"I'm sorry, lad. 'Tis na possible for even the best o' us. The veil gave that changelin' ta the horde those many years ago, an' it seems it's takin' him back today."

Cole shook. His mouth opened and closed, but he could not speak.

"Nuts to that!" a voice cried.

Chief Nudd turned his head. Cole looked up.

At the end of the platform stood Fable, her jaw squared and hands clenched in fists.

"Fable, no!" the queen yelled.

And then Fable punched the universe.

When the last of the goblin cliffs had vanished from view, Tinn sagged. He could feel the gentle ebb and flow tugging him toward the Annwyn, then back toward Earth. He closed his eyes and let himself hang in the empty space, swaying like a broken puppet.

The tug at his chest grew more urgent. He wondered if it would be like this for all eternity, the push and pull fighting against each other. Except it was more than just a tug now—something had changed. He felt his whole body being wrenched forward. Tinn opened his eyes.

A hand, a real hand, had him by the shirtfront. The mist faded and a pair of brilliant hazel eyes peered straight at him. Fable grinned, her grip tightened, and she yanked him toward her. Tinn could feel the magical current redoubling its efforts, the invisible string squeezing his ribs until he thought they would burst. Fable pulled.

The thin place shook.

Tinn grimaced against the pain. His bones felt as though they were rattling apart. He clutched the girl's arm tight with both of his goblin hands. Fable pulled again.

And then, with a clap like thunder, the unnatural fog vanished and the two of them landed on the goblin platform in a gasping, panting pile.

The cliffs exploded in noise as hundreds of goblins cheered and whooped and threw things into the air. Fable pushed her dark curls out of her eyes. "Take that, universe," she said. "Hi, Tinn!"

"Hi." Tinn laughed. "You—you saved me!"

"Of course I did."

Tinn had only just gotten to his feet when he was bowled over again by Cole, and in another moment they were both scooped up by their mother. Tears once more fell from Tinn's eyes, and when he reached a hand up to wipe them away, he froze, staring at his arm.

"Hey! You look like you!" said Cole.

"I look like—" Tinn turned his hands over and over and wiggled his fingers. They had lost their drab gray and were back to their usual dirty pink. "I look like me! I mean—I look like you!"

"We look like us," said Cole.

Tinn glanced up at the goblin chief. "How?"

Nudd shook his head, bewildered.

Kull clapped his hands. *"Kin an' kind!* That's what it says! The scroll says a changelin' will turn back ta *kin an' kind* when the magic has run its course. Doesn'a say *goblin-kind*. That's you lot, then. Yer the lad's—" He paused. His eyes met Tinn's and then dropped to the ground. "Yer the lad's true family."

Tinn stood, dumbstruck. "Does that mean I can—I can go home?"

Chief Nudd put a hand on the boy's shoulder. "Aye, lad. I believe it does."

"Well. What'ya say?" Kull smiled a crooked, toothy grin that, for all its horrifying angles, Tinn was beginning to find rather endearing. "I took a midnight trip wi' ya once, a long time ago, back when I started all this mess. What's say I take ya back again, one last time, an' see it done?"

THIRTY-SIX

Perhaps it was the glow of the predawn light just beginning to peek through the trees, but the Wild Wood did not feel quite as foreboding as the group traveled back through the forest toward town. Kull led the way, this time sticking faithfully to the old goblin paths. He said very little during the journey. Occasionally he hazarded a glance back. Although he smiled each time, his eyes were rimmed with red.

The goblin bridge was a narrow, winding strip of earth. As they crossed it, lights twinkled through the mist and reflected in the murky waters of the Oddmire. The hinky-punks kept their distance, but something told Cole that they were saying goodbye in their own way. Candlebeard separated himself from the procession, bowed low, and hopped across the water to join them.

"Goodbye," Cole called after him.

As they passed through the Wild Wood, they began to notice more eyes following their progress. A lithe fox crept up over a log, pausing to sit in plain sight as they walked by. A silvery white stag lifted its head to watch from the bushes. All around them, creatures of the forest had come to observe their march. Fable pointed eagerly as a pair of twinkling creatures with wings like dragonflies' peered at them through the branches.

"Hey! You came back!" she yelled, bounding into the bushes after them. "You came back and you stayed! Wait! Can I touch your wings? I'm really good at being gentle!"

The queen shook her head. She was smiling softly when she turned to the twins. "The forest is grateful for what you have done. The Wild Wood has grown accustomed to being a place of magic. Kull was right. It was becoming something less without it."

"It just needed a little," murmured Tinn. "Just enough."

The queen nodded. "I owe you a great debt for what you have done, changeling. You will always be welcome in the Wild Wood."

"Thanks. It's nice to know I can be safe here."

"Safe? That isn't remotely what I said. But you are most welcome. Now, I'm afraid it is time for us to leave you. We have much to do. The bramble is dead, but it must still be pulled up by its roots to ensure it does not return. And that Thing—"

"I let it escape," Tinn said. "I'm so sorry."

"I don't think that you did," said the queen. "Not completely. You showed kindness to the monster. A Thing like that will not easily be free of such a gesture." She looked over her shoulder into the green woods behind her. "If it ever shows itself in my forest again, however, I cannot promise that I will be as merciful."

Fable bounded back to the path, panting. "I touched a pixie's hair! And teeth. Well, it bit me. It bit me for touching its hair. It was so soft. And then pointy. My finger is kinda tingly now."

"Come, Fable," said the queen. She stepped off the goblin path, not waiting to see that her daughter was behind her. "It's time."

"Awww," Fable groaned.

"Just a moment," Annie said, letting go of her boys for the first time since they had begun the journey home. She knelt down and put a hand on Fable's arm. "Thank you, young lady. You gave me my sons back. I can't tell you what that means to me."

"Were you really gonna take me in," Fable asked, "if my mama wasn't my mama?"

Annie grinned. "It would have been my pleasure. I don't think there's any mother in the world who will look after you like yours, though. She's a very special mother. And you're a very special young woman. You can still come and visit us anytime, if you like."

Fable beamed. "Oh! Can I, Mama? Can I go to the people city? Sometimes? Just for a little while?"

The queen stiffened. "That would be severely ill advised."

Fable nearly vibrated with excitement. "So, *yes?*"

"Not remotely *yes.*"

"But not technically *no!*"

The queen sighed.

Fable turned around, beaming, and gave Annie Burton a bear hug that nearly tipped the woman over, and then bounded to the twins and hugged them each in turn.

"So, we're actual, real friends now, forever and ever and ever, right?" she said, her eyebrows rising so high they vanished into her curls.

"Friends," Tinn confirmed. "Forever and ever and ever."

"And we can keep saying things out loud to each other in people words? And maybe do a game or play a sports?"

"Of course," Cole laughed. "We would love to play sometime."

"Yesss." Fable spun on her heel and hopped after her mother. "Goodbye for now, friends! I'll see you tomorrow!"

"You most certainly will not. We have much to attend to, Fable," the queen was saying as they slid between the trees. "And what have I told you about pixies?"

"To not poke them when they don't want to be poked."

"And when do they want to be poked?"

"Not ever?"

"Correct."

"Sorry, Mama. I have friends now, though. Did you hear?" Fable's singsong voice carried through the forest. "People friends. Forever friends."

Soon their voices faded into the rustle and hum of the forest.

The rest of the trip was brief. Kull brought them right to the edge of the forest. Across the stream they could see the old climbing tree, and peeking over the rise was the roof of their house.

"There y'are," Kull said. "Safe an' sound. An' na more spyin' on ya, I promise. Nor attemptin' ta kidnap ya an' sell ya ta the fairies. Na even a little bit from now on."

Annie scowled, but she let it pass.

"Oh, an' one more thing, 'fore I go." Kull took a deep

breath. What came next emerged in a rush. "Yer a good mum, Annie Burton," he said. "Been watchin' a long time, so I'm sure. I only spent an hour wit' my changelin' an' I near ruined the wee thing's life forever. Ya been raisin' the twain, all by yer lonesome, fer years, an' every day ya turn their chaos inta somethin' special. Yer no goblin, but ya might be a better goblin than me. Yer sure a better parent." When he was done he gnawed on his bottom lip.

Annie stared. "Thank you," she managed at last.

"Thanks for everything, Mr. Kull," said Cole. He held out his hand. Startled and a little uncertain, Kull shook it.

Tinn came forward next. Kull shuffled his feet. "Well. Yer free o' me now," he said to his toes. "I'm sorry fer messin' up yer life, lad. Just . . . just be careful iffin ya do go back inta these woods. Witchy's blessing or na, there's still plenty that'll eat ya in here. An' mind that ya don't let that brother o' yorn talk ya inta anythin' too cockamamy. An' dinna give yer mothern too much trouble. But, ya know, do give her a bit." He chuckled meekly. "Yer still a goblin underneath, after all. Got a heritage ta remember."

"I've been thinking about that, actually," said Tinn.

Kull raised his eyes.

"If it's all right with my mom," Tinn said, "I think I'd like to learn more."

"More?"

"More about myself. About goblins. About where I came from. If you wouldn't mind. Not right away, but maybe someday I could visit? Just for a little while."

Kull's eyes widened, and they both looked at Annie.

Her brow creased and she looked wary. "Well," she began, "it might not hurt to understand a little more, but—"

"Oh, aye! There's na goblin in the horde who'd be happier ta teach ya a thing or two about our lot!" Kull was rocking back and forth on his feet, his eyes glossy with excitement. "Learnt a good bit more myself in the years since ya were born. Been collectin' books an' papers an' all manner o' such ta be learnin' from."

"We can discuss it," Annie conceded.

Kull remained watching from the bushes beside the stream as Annie Burton and her boys finally marched up the path toward home.

Back in their bedroom, with the dust and grime rinsed from their hair and their bellies full of potatoes and green beans and, at long last, several scrumptious marmalade tarts each, Tinn and Cole settled in to compare scars by the light of the rising sun.

"What about this one?" Tinn pulled up one leg of his

pajamas to show off a scrape that ran nearly the length of his shin.

"Ohhh. Nice," Cole marveled. "Check out the bruise on my knee."

"That's a good one."

When they had finished taking inventory of their injuries, they were silent for a while. They felt a strange fascination at being different for the first time in their lives.

Their mother came in shortly afterward to kiss them good night half a dozen times each before drawing the curtains closed against the morning light and ordering them to get some sleep.

Birds chirped in the field outside. In the dim golden haze, Tinn silently unwrapped the bandage from his hand. The bite was barely visible, although his palm was still tender. He turned his hand this way and that, gazing at his own skin.

"Hey, Cole," he whispered. "Are you awake?"

Cole's heavy breathing was his only reply. Tinn decided not to wake him. He couldn't blame his brother for being exhausted.

He turned his attention back to his hand. He never again had to fear looking down to see someone else's fingers at the end of his arms. Whatever magic had been inside him had gone back to where it belonged—that was how Nudd had explained it. Changeling magic was not meant to last forever.

If only he had known how to use his power when he still had it. What wonderful madness might transforming have added to their daily mischief? He held his breath for a minute, listening to the quiet house. Tinn concentrated, tensing his arm.

For a moment, just a fraction of an instant, his fingers flickered to the exact color of the woolly blanket beside him. Tinn's eyes widened, and a smile crept across his face. Tomorrow was going to be an interesting day.

EPILOGUE

CHIEF NUDD BREATHED IN DEEP, TAKING IN THE smell of the forest and the sight of the old cabin. He had left his usual entourage of lieutenants behind. This trip was for Nudd, alone. He had been a much younger goblin the last time he had come to this place.

"What are you doing here, thief king?" There was no warmth in the voice that greeted Nudd.

"I met her, ya know," the chief answered, conversationally. "Right here. Many times. Yer mother was a fine woman, witch."

The Queen of the Deep Dark eyed Nudd bitterly as she stepped into the light. "You knew my mother?"

"Aye."

"And you let her die alone in the woods." The witch's voice was as soft and as cold as a fresh snowfall. "We are not friends, you and I."

Nudd chuckled softly. "Na a soul on this earth *let* yer mother do anythin', lass. She did or she didn'a as she pleased. Force o' nature, that one. I believe she stayed because she was waitin'."

"Don't call me *lass*," said the queen. Nudd could see waves of emotion rolling just behind her stony countenance. "Waiting?" she added. "For what?"

"Fer ya."

"It would be unwise to toy with me, thief king."

"She loved ya, lass."

"I said don't call me—"

"She loved ya, Raina."

The Queen of the Deep Dark froze. "What did you say?"

"Yer name. She said it often enough. I 'spect ya probably dinna remember it, ya were such a wee little thing when we—"

"I remember." The queen stared at Nudd, although something in her eyes told him what she was seeing was infinitely farther away. When she spoke again, the ice had begun to melt away from her words. "You really knew her?"

Nudd nodded.

"Will you—" She hesitated. "Will you tell me about her?"

Nudd considered for a moment. "That child o' yorn. Fable, is it? She crossed inta the veil last night. She took hold o' the very fabric o' the universe, an' when she had it in her hands, she shook it. That's the spirit o' yer mother, right there."

The queen, Raina, smiled in spite of herself.

At the same moment, Nudd's own grin vanished. "A human should na have survived that. A human *could* na have survived that. I'll tell ya anythin' ya want ta know about yer mother, witch." His eyes narrowed. "If ya tell me about the girl."

ACKNOWLEDGMENTS

RESEARCH FOR THIS BOOK BEGAN A LONG TIME ago, with a different pair of troublemaking boys tromping through the trees in search of impossible things. I want to thank Alex Reisfar for filling the forests of my childhood with magic. I haven't stopped tromping.

There are good people in the world who do difficult work, navigating the real Deep Dark to help lost children find their way through the shadows and back into the light of day. I would also like to thank Erin Farrell for walking that path. Without her, our story might never have been.

And, as ever, I cannot adequately express my gratitude for Katrina, the most indomitable force of nature I have ever met. If you look for her in this story, you will find her. Her hands have brushed the leaves of the Wild Wood, and the forest has grown more vibrant at her touch.